Leave a Light on for Christmas

by

Barb Bissonette

Strategic Book Publishing and Rights Co.

Strategic Book Publishing and Rights Co.
12620 FM 1960, Suite A4-507
Houston, TX 77065
www.sbpra.com

ISBN 978-1-62212-312-4

Dedication

This book is dedicated to my husband, John,
with whom I have spent many happy Christmases–
enough to tell a story on a Christmas tree

"My Christmas tree tells a story," I whispered softly into the tiny, perfectly shaped ear of my new baby great-granddaughter.

She was only three-and-a-half weeks old and she looked as if she'd been fashioned straight from the hand of God. She was flawless. Her skin was smooth and sweet and she had that newborn smell that is the most beautiful smell in the entire world. She was my very first great-grandchild and she was named after me. I was seventy-six years old and I thought that I was too old to experience the degree of joy and complete bliss which Hannah had delivered to me single-handedly just a few weeks before Christmas. But apparently I was not too old at all.

Everyone had gone out to a Christmas gathering and I was in charge of baby Hannah. It was my pleasure. She was very sweet natured and rarely cried. When she woke up she looked around with her huge, clear eyes which were still, of course, a dark shade of blue, and I could see the lights from my tree reflected with multi-coloured illumination in them. We were sitting beside the tree, she and I, in my old, old rocker where I had rocked my babies and my grandbaby, and any others who had come to call and needed a bit of comfort.

"Oh, yes. My Christmas tree tells a story. It's the story of my life, you see. It's like a big old book with different chapters and all the years in between. I've kept all of my ornaments. I couldn't bear to throw any of them out, wee Hannah. It's an old story that's been a long time in the telling, but it's all here. I can sit right here with you, my little love, and think about all those years. Some were good and some were bad and some were wonderful and some–not many, but some–were just awful. But you have to put them all together. You can't leave any out. It's my whole story, the entire thing, and every year at Christmas I take them out and put them all together on my Christmas tree. It's my life."

I tucked her into my arms ever so gently and kissed the softness of her sweet cheek.

"It started in 1935."

I let myself sink into the chair and remember–down, down through the calendar of days that had grown together and become my life.

There were significant things about 1935–besides being my birth year, of course. It was a whole other world back then. I wonder sometimes if we'd known how the world would go–how things would change so much in every single aspect of life–if we would have had the courage to keep going. I guess that's why we do go on, though. It's because things change a little at a time until you're in another place that has gradually been altered bit by bit until nothing is recognizable from the start. But you don't see the little bits changing as you go along, day by day.

My mother, my dear, dear mother, was actually, I think, years ahead of her time. She could have been a Hallmark mascot with her Christmas ornaments. I mean, nowadays it's customary to mark each year with a new ornament, proudly displaying the year and marking such occasions as births and weddings and new homes, etc. But in 1935 it was almost unheard of. People were interested in keeping body and soul together and food on the table.

It was after World War I–the Great War– ("What's so great about it?" my grandfather used to say to anyone who would listen) and the world was brewing for the second war. Adolf Hitler was stirring up trouble overseas in Germany. It was the year that he adopted for Nazi Germany a new national flag sporting the swastika. And we all know how that ended. It was the year that Parker Brothers released the board game Monopoly. It was also the year of the screening of *Snow White and the Seven Dwarfs* which was the first feature-length animated movie.

All of these things were of great importance, in varying degrees, to the world. But my mom overlooked all of these things. She sat down at her kitchen table in the midst of all of this political turmoil which was bombarding the radios and newspapers, and made a Christmas ornament commemorating my first Christmas. As aforementioned, this is a common practice nowadays but not so much then. That is the first ornament that I hang on my tree each year, and I always wrap it up with great care in tissue paper when I dismantle it. I don't think there are too many people my age who can boast of a "baby's first Christmas" ornament from the year 1935. After I've unearthed that ornament I always feel as if she is still with me every Christmas– that the love with which she fashioned it has lingered and has become a tangible thing that I can fasten onto a pine branch.

It's very simple, really. Even by those old time standards it is not particularly elegant, but to me it is priceless. Its underlying form is unknown to me as it is covered completely by little squares of all different coloured bits of material. I suspect that they were scraps, but I don't know for sure. They were glued all over this ball and then reinforced with multiple layers of binder twine. I know that it doesn't sound elegant but it has a unique beauty to it, probably because it is so old and antiquated looking. If nothing else, it is very colourful. Over the top of all these bits of colours were painted the words, "Hannah's First Christmas" in dark red, and a little flannel, flesh-colored cutout of a baby lay underneath the words. It is hard for me to believe that this ornament is 76 years old. It is still in fine form as it clings together and glorifies my tree after all this time.

"We have a new ornament for you, my dear," I whispered to my small namesake, rocking her gently and tenderly as we both gazed at the shining lights-and the baby's first Christmas ball featured on a prominent branch. "You're part of my life story now. This is the very first year for your Christmas ball-and one of my last, I think." I sighed deeply and thought of the infinite, circle of life.

I thought of my mother and how much love she had infused into that little Christmas ball and how her love has lived on and on in me. And every time I hang that ball up I can feel her so close to me, as if she were my very own Christmas angel.

1935 was a long, long time ago and I know that any stories which I recalled from then were only mine because they had been repeated to me, and repeated so often that they became, in turn, my own memories. You know how that goes? You hear a story so many times that you are quite sure that indeed you do remember it.

My first Christmas was like that. It had to have been like that, of course, because I was only four months old. But when I shut my eyes and think really hard I can feel it inside of me–that first-ever Christmas of mine.

It was hard times in the world, as I've mentioned. Canada was on the brink of war, even as it was recovering from the last one. My father was a farmer and worked like a Trojan every day of his life. There are no days off when you are a farmer. My mother worked hard, too. She had chickens, and she often went out to do chores when my father was busy in the fields. This I know for a fact from my firsthand knowledge. But the rest of my memory–the first Christmas part–was from my father telling me over the years.

It was this Christmas, my first Christmas, when my mother began the tradition of lighting a candle in a mason jar and leaving it burning in the snow bank at the end of our lane. She did this every Christmas Eve thereafter. Many of these I do have actual memories of, of course and as I got bigger I helped her light it.

But the story of my first Christmas I remember particularly because my father told me of it many times. He recalled how she had unearthed a mason jar and a long tapered candle. She was searching for matches when she asked him to bundle me up in my bunting bag.

"What on earth for?"

"We have to leave a light on for Christmas. We have to walk down to end of our lane."

Our long country lane was a half-mile long and the night was bitter cold.

"For Christmas?"

"Yes. For Baby Hannah, of course. Come on, Henry." She pulled him along with her mittened hand. "It's her very first Christmas. We have to leave a light in the world for her."

1939

The next date that I should have had on my tree is 1939. This is the year that my sister Agnes was born. It was so wonderful for me. I truly can remember how great it was to have a brand new baby sister. People don't believe that so much anymore. Nobody remembers when they were five years old, but I am here to tell you that I do. Agnes was born on September 1st, 1939. Anybody who knows anything at all about history will know that this was the day that sparked the beginning of the Second World War. This was the day when Germany invaded Poland without warning, which had the consequences of Britain and France being at war with them within two days, and Australia, Canada and South Africa within a week.

I have heard the story many, many times and I am always glad that I have my very own bit of history happening on that same day. I remember more than the actual birth of Agnes. I recall the feeling of having a sister to love in the world, someone who was made just like me, from the same Mom and Dad, and would share my home and my childhood years. Someone who was priceless.

I don't, of course, remember much about the war years–just what was told to me–but I don't ever remember a Christmas in that old, rambling farmhouse that wasn't happy and loving. People have shared stories with me as an adult of those years and how hard things were and how downtrodden their families were. I cannot participate in these reminiscences as I have no memory of such. That is not to say my parents were not desperately worried and upset at times, but they did not pass this on to us. My Christmas memories of old were of Mom on the piano playing the ancient Christmas carols and singing and laughing in time to the music; of neighbours dropping in and always being offered baking and a glass of Dad's homemade wine.

Dad didn't have to go to war as he was needed on the farm. I was all grown up before I realized that a great big "Thank God" was warranted for that, as I saw the effect the war had had on my classmates' fathers–the ones who died over there and the ones who lived to struggle for life back home.

We didn't ever have any money in my growing-up years, but it just didn't matter one bit. We had nothing, but neither did anyone else, which is why it didn't matter. We all just had nothing and we were okay with that. When I say "nothing," I'm talking about material goods and actual cash. I am not talking about food and warmth and love. Those we had in spades.

The Christmas ornament that was Agnes's first one has been misplaced over the years. I gave my sister trouble for this, as I could not imagine losing anything as precious as such a thing, but she was always very casual about things like this . She thought that I was just a silly old packrat and that she didn't need the ornament to remind her of Mama's love. I would have died if I hadn't had mine even for one year, but hers got lost somewhere in the midst of her moving one of her lives in exchange for another. Perhaps that was why I never misplaced anything like that. I always held on so very hard to my life and never got uprooted. I had deep roots even as a young girl. Aggie, on the other hand, had expansive wings. It's funny how that goes.

But sufficient to say that she had a "baby's first" ornament at one time and that I can remember it shining away on the pine branches beside mine–quite similar, really, just different letters and different materials. Other than that they were quite alike. Two peas in a pod. Two girls from the same parents–the same DNA, the same genes. Two girls as different as night and day. But still two souls with a bond as deep and abiding as the old farm itself.

I may have only a memory of Aggie's baby ball. I do, however, have an ornament dated 1947 that has been mine for sixty years or more (very formidable thought.) I guess that Aggie is right and I am a packrat, but Mama taught us, too, the value of these old things which were once so very loved. She took the time and effort to fashion these ornaments and she taught us how important it is to remember things.

The 1947 ornament was a square cardboard thing with a picture on the front cover of *The Diary of a Young Girl* on it. It must have been an advertisement which she cut out and glued on and wrote on the back of. It's funny how you don't think of these things so much when you're a kid. You just take them for granted, but I realize now what an impact this story had on my mom. Maybe because she had two little girls of her own. Mom was always someone who counted herself lucky to live on a Canadian farm where she was free and happy, and so she felt keenly the imprisonment of a fourteen-year-old girl's spirit. When I was older I had this cardboard ornament laminated to preserve it and how glad I am now that I did.

There on the back of the photo of a raven-haired girl with a tenuous smile were written these words in my mother's handwriting:

"In 1945 Anne Frank died at the age of 14 in a Nazi concentration camp. She kept this diary while she was hiding in the attic of an Amsterdam home. One of her last entries noted her conviction that all people are basically good. Her book has been published in 1947."

I knew that this last sentence in itself would mean everything to Mama who, as well, believed in the inherent goodness of mankind.

I didn't always see things her way and I didn't always agree, but it was good for your soul to have a mom who did believe in the inherent goodness of people. When I think of her it always gladdens my heart just a little to remember that for her, goodness abounded in the world-no matter what the world tried to do to prove otherwise.

I don't remember exactly how old I was when I first saw the movie *It's a Wonderful Life*. I think that it originally aired in 1946, but I don't know for sure if I saw it then.

And in those days not everyone had a television set–certainly not farmers who were barely scratching a living out of the tough Ontario soil. But gradually, it has become a part of my whole Christmas repertoire of memories. Because no matter when it came on, Mama would stop whatever she was doing, dry her hands on her ever-present apron and sit with Agnes and me to watch it in its entirety. This was way, way before the days of DVD and VHS and if you wanted to watch something you consulted the *TV Guide* to ascertain when your program would be airing. And if you didn't sit and watch it, then you simply missed it. And that was that.

But from the time that I was probably about thirteen or so one of the highlights of my Christmas season was to watch *It's a Wonderful Life* snuggled up on the ancient comfortable chesterfield with Mom and Aggie. It was one of the very few times that Mama was still with quiet hands. She loved that movie and she taught us to love it, too. I think that the nicest part of that memory was just being with her. We would roast chestnuts in foil on the old fireplace and usually have a cup of milky tea. Mom would snuggle us up beside her and sigh with deep pleasure as the movie started with the stars [supposedly angels] talking and trying to solve the problem of a very discouraged man, George Bailey, who didn't want to live any more. Mom always said that this story was really about an answer to a prayer. The angel Clarence was the answer to his prayer, presumably to show George what the world would have been like if he'd never been born, thus making him want to live again. Mama never ceased to let us know how special life was and how every single person makes a mark on this big old world.

"Imagine a world without a Hannah," she would say as she hugged me close to her and kissed my head. "Or a dear little Aggie." And she would, in turn, kiss Agnes's head.

"It just wouldn't bear thinking about."

No wonder we learned to love the movie so much. We each felt very special.

That was when I fell in love with Jimmy Stewart, and I never quite got over that. I used to dream that I was Donna Reed and that I was getting to kiss the tall, gangly, kind hero of the story. Kindness was always the most important thing to me in any person, man or woman. Mama taught us that every day of our lives but never so much as when we were all as one on the old couch watching our favorite story of the season.

"Just look at him," she would say, year after year, as if we'd never seen the tale before. "Just look at him giving up his chance to travel and see the world."

"You gotta love Jimmy Stewart," my dad would call from the kitchen where he sat contentedly by the table, reading the *Farmers Almanac* and smoking his beloved pipe.

"I do love him, Henry. I do, indeed," Mom would call back, her voice full of laughter.

"He was a war hero, you know. He fought for our country for four-and-a-half years. He was an actor before the war and he's just getting back into it now. But he didn't want anything mentioned about his war record. He's very humble."

"How do we know this then, Beth? I'm asking you."

"I know this because I have eyes and ears and read newspapers and think about something other than chores and cows, that's how."

He always laughed then and shook his head, saying, "Well, you girls watch your Jimmy Stewart then, and I'll just sit here with my pipe, and I expect we'll all be happy as kings, so we will."

So Mama pulled us closer to her than ever and continued with her narrative of George Bailey's life. I'm sure to this day I could recite every line in that movie.

And at the end when everyone brings money and Christmas wishes and the strains of "Auld Lange Syne" fill the TV screen, Mama always sang, too. And she always had tears streaming down her face because she did so like happy endings, my mom.

"Lest old acquaintance be forgot
And never brought to mind.
Lest old acquaintance be forgot
And days of auld Lang Syne."

Somewhere along the line during one of those Christmas seasons, we made an *It's a Wonderful Life* ornament. Again, Mama must have found an advertisement in a magazine or something because she carefully cut out a photograph of George Bailey lifting Mary up high over his head. She is looking down at him and they are both laughing. She is wearing red shoes and a red blouse and I thought she looked perfect. Not to mention lucky as hell to have Jimmy Stewart holding her up in the air. I thought it would be the best thing in the world to have a man lift you up in the air so high that you just had to laugh from the sheer joy of it.

Agnes and I took the picture and formed it around a paper mache ball that I had lovingly molded out of homemade glue and old newspaper. Agnes, I think, thought that I was a little cracked in the head when I produced this. She loved the movie, too, but she didn't love Mr. Stewart with quite the degree of intensity that I did. Actually, Agnes didn't have quite the same degree of intensity of feeling as I did for most things in life.

We got some little feathers from the chicken coop and glued them on the sides for wings. They lasted surprisingly well, too. Even now you can see some tufts of feathers clinging to the top of the worn-out ball. And Mama found a little jingle bell that we tied onto the top, thus completing the ensemble. So it was all set to ring upon any movement as it resided on the pine branches.

"Every time a bell rings, an angel gets his wings."

This is, of course, the whole point to the story. George's angel ends up getting his wings by saving George from a watery grave as the whole town [plus my mama] sing "Auld Lang Syne."

I could never ever hear that song without holding back tears.

For the melody.

For the story.

For my mom.

Nowadays it would be foolish indeed to think that you would end up for the rest of your days with the fellow that you started going out with when you were just a teenager. Nowadays eighteen is considered very young and women are not even through school or aware of what they want to do with their lives. Women have careers and they travel all over the globe. It is not unusual to start bearing children in their thirties, even forties. Looking back at all of this from a lofty old age of seventy-six, I think that this is all very well for the members of my sex. I think that the more you can do to broaden your horizons and see everything you can, the better it is for you.

But the world was a very different place when I was eighteen. It was 1953 and the whole wide world was still in a state of recovery from the assault of World War II. I had been working for a year to help supplement the family expenses, during the summer and after school in the spring and fall at the local Dominion Seed House.

The Dominion Seed House was on Highway #7 in Georgetown, and it had been there as long as I could ever remember. I had always loved the look of it. It was black and white and was done in a mock Tudor style–very distinctive and very impressive. That building was a landmark for people for many, many years. People used to visit from all over to look at the unusual buildings and to see where their seeds came from, for we shipped the seeds all over Canada-even then.

That building was sold in 1998 and demolished in 1999. I cried and cried when they knocked it down. It had so many memories for me. And I loved that it was there–just there on the side of the road. Just there where it was supposed to be. Like something good and solid that you could depend on.

I met my Hank there. I was working hard. Children raised on a farm are usually good workers. We were taught the value of an honest day's work and we believed in it. The Dominion Seed House was largely a mail order business. On an average day in the busy summer months, 3000 orders would arrive each day and they all had to be manually filled. This did not leave a lot of time to spare. But I was a normal, eighteen-year-old girl and the passionate blood of my forefathers ran through my veins. The new employee was a tall, dark-haired boy with soulful eyes and a quick easy manner of working who caught my eye without too much trouble. I didn't know him at all, but my ears were pricked open to the snippets of gossip that ran through the seed house at lunch and coffee break. He was from northern Ontario and was working his way across Canada, boarding with a local farmer. The word around the lunch room was that he was helping with the chores to pay for his room and board. I listened nonchalantly as others around me put in their two cents' worth. His name was Hank Moreau. His father was a drunk, and Hank had fled his isolated northern home to set out on his own. He was a good worker and the bosses were all very pleased with him and hoped that he'd stay for a while–over the busy season anyway. He was shy and hadn't spoken too much but was friendly when approached. He cut across the fields at the back of DSH to hurry home in time to help Old Man O'Halloran with his chores. He had a pair of the softest, kindest brown eyes in the world. Oh, wait–that was my two cents.

I was very shy, especially as a young girl, and the wonder of my whole life is that Hank and I did manage to spark up a conversation at all. It was all more good luck than good management, really. I like to think that it was fate. I helped fate along just a little, tiny bit by starting to cut across the back way home through the fields myself.

I'd heard in the rumblings of gossip that abound anywhere when more than two women work together that this was his daily route. So I thought that I might start walking that way as well. I told Mom it was to save time, and I told myself that too. And I almost believed it.

And the rest, as they say, is history. It was a long, hot summer and we were young and happy. So very, very happy. There never has been anything in the world that poets anywhere have found to compare with young love.

The first place that Hank and I ever went was to see the show in nearby Brampton. I can recall to this day how nervous I was. Old Man O'Halloran had lent Hank his car and he came to pick me up, winding up the long old dusty lane and looking just like the answer to any prayer that I'd ever made.

Mama liked him right away, as she did most folk. Dad was more hesitant but had to admit that he'd heard from Old Man O'Halloran that he was a hard worker, so this was in Hank's favour. To my Dad if you weren't a hard worker there was just "no use of you." Mama thought that he had a kind, rugged face. I didn't care about the rugged bit [not exactly sure what that meant], but I cared deeply about the kindness.

We went to see *Gentlemen Prefer Blondes*. Marilyn Monroe was in that movie and it depicted two gals from Little Rock making the big time in Paris. She was so beautiful and sexy. I said this to Hank, but he said that I was the most beautiful girl that he'd ever seen. Since I really was quite plain and wearing a ragged skirt with a well-worn sleeveless blouse I thought that maybe this fellow–this tall, rugged fellow with the big shoulders and the twinkling eyes and the shy quiet manner about him–was falling for me. Maybe.

I can remember the complete and utter happiness that engulfed me as I crept into my bunk bed that night, with Aggie breathing rhythmically below me, as she always did. I felt surrounded by love in a totally different way than I had for all of my life in my farmhouse home. And it never left me. I was one of the lucky ones. I found my love and I held onto him for dear life. For that was my way. I held things dear and kept them close.

If I hadn't, I wouldn't have a whole tree worth of ornaments to whisper about in the ear of this new Hannah.

We were engaged by September. People did not wait long in those days. What was the point?

And that Christmas there was a new ornament on the tree. Mama had made it and it became mine, but for that year it hung on the tree in the old farm. Can you guess what it was? Anybody?

If you had ever known my mom you would have figured it out. It was a miniature building fashioned from little sticks and painstakingly painted in the Tudor style of black and white.

DSH was painted on the front door and underneath was the message in old ball point ink: "Christmas 1953

Where it all began

Georgetown, Ontario."

Tiny Hannah, so wonderful and sweet, was now sleeping soundly in my arms, sleeping as only ones who are very new can. She was so new that I felt as if she was still somewhat clinging to that other world from which she had tumbled and landed firmly and securely into our family circle of love. Into her little spot in the big old world of today, a spot which had been always open just for her and which now welcomed her as a long-awaited treasure. I'm sure the angels could still reach down and whisper in her tiny ears, so new was she. And I–well, I was old now and I was happy to just rock her and hold her. I had always taken my duties as a mother and grandmother very seriously and had fulfilled lots of obligations along the path of being both. But this was different. All that I was required to do for this little thing was to love her. And that, well, that I could do. I'd had lots and lots of practice at loving. And this little girl child was very loveable indeed.

I was still rocking, very, very softly and I kept telling my story. I wanted her to hear it-her and her angels who were gently setting her free to her new life. The story of my Christmas tree: the story of my life.

It wasn't an extraordinary story. It didn't depict great adventure or great riches. It was, on the contrary, a rather ordinary story, I'm sure, by most people's standards. But it was mine and I loved it. I loved it enough to take it out each December and caress it lovingly and hang it with pride all over the pine branches. My life in Christmas ornaments.

I snuggled Hannah closer to me and kissed her perfect face and kept on with my saga. By now I knew that the telling was intended not just for her, but for me, as well.

I smiled to myself.

In those days, of course, people did not live together before marriage. It just wasn't done. I did not know, nor had I ever known, anyone at all who had lived together without first being wed. Nor did I, personally, know anyone who was divorced. I knew *of* people, but nowhere in my small world of south-western Ontario had divorce been so much as mentioned. This was not to say that everyone was blissfully happy with his or her counterpart. Some were decidedly unhappy. But that just wasn't the point. You married for better or for worse and that was that. I think really that it's all just a matter of luck more than anything if you marry your true love. And, as I said already, I was one of the lucky ones. So was my Mama.

Hank and I were married at the old farm house on New Year's Day 1954. We had been engaged for five months. It was a small wedding. We had no extra money, but Mama put on a spread fit for a king. My dad always said that she was the best cook in the world, and she could make a feast out of next to nothing. She'd made my wedding cake too, although she would have liked more time for it to "cure." But Mama was clever enough to note the way that we looked at each other. She was also clever enough to see that she just wasn't getting any more time. We couldn't wait. I remember the wedding cake recipe because you had to use rosewater, which was something I couldn't fathom. But it tasted heavenly.

Mama had left the Christmas garlands and tree up by way of decorations. Well, partly for decoration and partly because she believed completely and firmly that it was bad luck to take your tree down before the New Year. She had scoured the nearby woods and cut down boughs of pine and the house smelled magnificent. She had made dozens of little candles by pouring paraffin wax into small jars and lighting them all over our large old fashioned living room.

I wore an ivory suit that Mama and I had made. Baby mums adorned my hair. Hank looked as handsome as any man could in his rented tuxedo. When I look at the old black and white photo that someone had remembered to snap, we don't look especially outstanding. But we sure do look happy.

There was a family photo taken on that day, also. It was quite small, really, when you think that it encompassed the whole family of the bride and the groom. Hank had not invited his father and so it was only he and I, Mama and Dad, and Agnes. Mama was always small. She was short and quite tiny, even as she got older. Dad used to brag that he could put his hands right around her waist. She escaped the dreaded "middle-aged spread" probably because she was never still long enough to keep weight on. She had auburn hair which was threaded with grey as long ago as I can remember. I always knew that she was beautiful because the girls from school used to tell me quite regularly. And I had the good fortune to take after my mother in looks–a fact that never ceased to delight me. Agnes, on the other hand, was tall and big boned and dark haired like our dad. This was the bane of her existence, but Mama used to tell her that you can't do anything at all about how you look, only about how you are inside. And she always told both of us that we were her beautiful girls. So did Dad, actually. It's a nice thing to remember.

The plan was for us to live at the old farm house with Mama and Dad until spring. Dad had given us four acres of land that faced north on the far side of the farm as a wedding gift. And as soon as the ground broke we would start building our very own house. I was in heaven.

Hank and I spent a weekend in Niagara Falls. After all, it was and still is the honeymoon capital of the world. Even though it has become a cliché I will always love the beauty and splendor of the magnificent falls. Hank had never seen them and was amazed at how close they were to our home. It was only a two-hour drive and we felt as if we were in a whole other world. We reveled in their thundering ruggedness as we reveled in wonder at the sheer joy of our love for each other.

We moved in with Mama and Dad and Agnes with surprising ease and eagerly awaited the breaking of the ground for our new home in the spring. I longed for a home of my own. I longed to be a proper wife with my own kitchen. I longed to sew curtains for my own windows where I could wait every day for my man to come over the fields and into our home . My big handsome loving man of whom I loved every inch. This was years before the women's liberation movement. I didn't know that I wasn't supposed to be happy just being a housewife. I was in seventh heaven.

It was nice, though, to go on living with Mama. I realized that Hank liked it as well. All of the mother in law jokes just didn't apply to us. We lived together in harmony. One night as we retired to bed and snuggled up under the quilt which Mama had hand sewn, we lay listening to her as she went through her little nighttime ritual. Her presence in the house was ever gentle and loving-even when you could only hear her.

"It's nice to be here with your folks," Hank whispered as he absentmindedly kissed my cheek. "Do you have any idea how sweet you mom really is?"

"Of course I do," I replied, surprised by the question. "She's great."

"She's more than great. She's amazing, Hannah. I never really had a mom, you know."

"I'm sorry, darling."

"Oh, don't be sorry. It doesn't matter. You don't miss what you don't have."

"You don't?"

"No. Not really. I mean you know that things aren't right but you just figure that's your lot in life. You know?"

I didn't really know. When you've always had stable, loving parents you just figure that is the norm. I'd never thought too much about the alternative.

"How old were you when your mom died?" I asked gently into the darkness.

"Eight."

"That's too young, Hank. That's too young to lose your mom."

He laughed softly.

"I know, my sweet. But these things aren't planned, you know. They just happen that way, is all."

I was starting to drop off, still marveling at how wonderful it felt to rest while encased in those big muscular arms, when Hank's words again broke the silence of the winter night.

"She was better off, you know."

These words startled me out of my half sleep.

"Better off?"

"Oh, yes. I knew that when she got sick she wouldn't fight too hard to hold onto life. He had broken her spirit so badly by then. He was a drunk, plain and simple,-and a mean drunk at that. The good days were the days when he got drunk and fell asleep. We would just tiptoe around, Mother and I-desperately not wanting to disturb him. She was tired and broken, my poor little Mom. When she got sick she just lay her head down on the pillow in relief, I'm sure."

"But surely she would want to live for you. You were her son."

"Oh, I think she did, in a way. But she'd lost her will along the way. She'd lost her joy. I mean, she had no money, no relatives of her own. There was no way out for her. We were way up in Timmins, surrounded by his cronies and drunk cousins. There was nowhere to go."

He sighed so deeply that I felt it right to the tip of his toes.

We were silent for a while as I pondered how different our young lives had been (for he was only two years older than I) and how absolutely lucky I was.

His next words reiterated this thought.

"I wasn't trying to feel sorry for myself, love. I'm just trying to say how much I appreciate the kindness of your folks. Especially your mama. Sometimes, like now when we can hear her downstairs putting the house in order, she seems like an angel almost. I like to think that's how my mom might have been if she'd had someone decent to be with her. He wouldn't have had to be rich or spectacular or even anything special, really. Just decent, you know."

We were both quiet as we heard Mama turn out the lights and softly climb upstairs, pausing at Aggie's room as she looked in on her for a last good night peek. Last year she would have looked in on me as well. I knew it–sometimes I had still been awake and I had heard her or felt the soft touch of her hand against my cheek. But not now, of course. That wouldn't have befitted a married woman at all. But I knew that she sent us an unspoken good night and blessing as she rounded the corner to the big old room at the end of the hall which she had shared with my dad since forever. I heard her get into bed beside my father.

The world was still.

And all was well.

People tend to remember world events by what was happening in their lives at that time. For instance, for many years in the '60s we were asking one another "What were you doing when President Kennedy was shot?" It's human nature, I'm sure.

"What were you doing on October 15, 1954?"

That was another question, particularly for those living in and around the Brampton area. That is a huge area now but in 1954 it consisted of only a few thousand people and we could all answer that question with no hesitation. Especially me.

On October 15 1954 I was giving birth.

As Hurricane Hazel ripped through southern Ontario, taking a toll of destruction and what turned out to be a total of eighty-one lives with it, I was bringing a little girl into the stricken world. The flooding was astronomical. Highway 10 was washed completely away.

My baby was born at Peel Memorial Hospital in Brampton. It had begun as the home of William Elliot who was an early settler to the area. It became Peel Memorial in 1925 and began as a memorial to the soldiers who had served their country in World War I. Georgetown didn't have a hospital until 1962, but it didn't matter too much to me. Brampton was only a scant eight miles east of us. Surely that was not too far. Not too far on any other day, true. But on this particular day, it turned out to be very far indeed.

Those were the days when you were on your own as soon as you were in labor. Now, the fathers are allowed in and other family members, but not so then. You were alone in a cold, white sterile room with an equally cold and sterile nurse. I was terrified and felt completely alone and helpless, not to mention uncertain of this whole process.

It's not that Mama was secretive about such things, like so many of her generation. And I'd lived on the farm long enough to know about birth and where babies came from. I didn't go into that white hospital world totally ignorant–quite the contrary–but it was still an overwhelming shock. The isolation–the starkness–the all-encompassing pain that felt as if it was ripping my body into two distinct halves. This was before epidurals and breathing exercises and spousal support. You just screamed and screamed until the pain took over entirely and tore your body apart. That is how it seemed to me, anyways.

I was just barely nineteen years old. Even though I was technically an adult and a wife, I was really not much more than a child myself.

I thought that the nurses were very stern and professional and without compassion at all. And perhaps they were. It wasn't until later that I discovered the total devastation which Hazel had left in her wake and how upset the whole world was on that day. Looking back, I'm sure that the nurses had much more on their minds than a little farm girl who was giving birth on their shift. In their eyes this was an everyday occurrence, nothing to get too excited about, just a necessary part of life. Quite a different thing for the one bearing her first child, I must say.

I had no idea until after my wee girl was safely in my arms what a national event Hurricane Hazel had become. She was relentless and merciless. She had killed as many as a thousand people in Haiti before striking the United States and causing another ninety-five fatalities. She caused the States $308 million in damages. She had traveled 680 miles over land but while approaching Canada had merged with an existing powerful cold front. Thus the storm stalled over the Toronto area, and although it was now extropical, it still was as powerful as a category one hurricane with gusts of over 93 miles per hour and rainfall up to eight inches. As she left Toronto the storm slowed from 48 miles per hour to eleven miles per hour all within the span of a day. She continued north through Ontario, passing over James Bay and reaching northern Quebec. She left devastation in her wake. Thousands of people lost their homes and all of their possessions while eighty-one people lost their lives. Thirteen of these were just small children. This was heartbreaking for Mama, who was tender hearted almost to a fault sometimes. But where children were concerned she was inconsolable.

I was allowed to go home earlier than was usual in those days because the hospital was bursting at the seams with casualties. I was glad to go home. Scared and sore and aching, but glad. I would rather have my own mom and sister any day to those taciturn nurses.

Mama rocked my new girl in the chair effortlessly as we all had tea and breathed a huge sigh of relief with her safe arrival and the departure of the hurricane.

"We are so glad you're here safe and sound, dear." She was whispering in my little girl's ear and alternately talking to Hank and Aggie and Dad and me as we gathered together, thankful to be able to do so.

She faced us and shuddered as she recalled the days which had preceded this calm one.

"Imagine that poor man crossing the bridge and having his child torn right out of his arms to drown. It doesn't bear thinking about."

"It's tough." Dad agreed, puffing on his old pipe. He wasn't usually allowed to do this inside any more but today my mom cared not about rules, so happy was she to have her family around her again—not to mention a brand-new granddaughter.

"There were whole families dead on Raymore Drive." Aggie said. "It says in the paper that there was a couple and their three children all dead. The baby was only three months old. And another family too with three small children. I don't know where Raymore Drive is but it seems like a lot of people died who lived on it."

"It's in Etobicoke, I think." Hank said. "Someone at work was talking about it."

"It's awful. Just awful."

It was something that the survivors of the mighty hurricane never forgot. I can remember now quite clearly [more clearly than some things much more recently] how we all felt completely beaten down by the results of Hazel who came through our land unbidden and left such destruction.

Mama was grateful–just grateful. She was so glad that our baby had arrived safely and that I was well. Those were the days when it was not unheard of to have a mother succumb to the perils of childbirth.

"What are you going to call this little girl?" My dad asked, gazing over at my mother who was totally engrossed in her tiny hands–ten fingers and ten toes. I had never realized that this in itself was a miracle.

"Mary," we said in unison.

"That's a good name," my father pronounced.

"After my mother," Hank said very softly.

"Even better," my father declared while my mother started to sing sweetly to the child in her arms an old song which I'd heard her sing before and many times since:

"For it was Mary, Mary was a grand old name
Mary plain as any name can be
But with propriety, society will say 'Marie'
But it was Mary, Mary long before the fashion came
And there is something there that sounds so square
It's a grand old name."

I saw my dad grin indulgently and a part of me marveled that he still was happy to hear her sing. She had lots of silly little tunes which she sang as she went about her life. She was singing this one with love and tenderness to the little girl who I knew would learn to adore her as I did.

"Mary what?" Agnes asked, ever practical.

Hank and I looked at each other and laughed. We hadn't got that far yet.

"What about Mary Hazel?" she suggested. "After all, it must be a big deal to be born on the day when *she* came. We've never had a hurricane before."

"I hope we never do again," I shuddered.

"That's what I mean. It's memorable."

"I heard that they're retiring that name from the use of North Atlantic hurricanes because of its death toll and how much damage it did," my father commented.

"How about Mary Hannah?" Hank asked, looking at me and smiling.

He nodded in the direction of my mother who was completely oblivious to all of these practical matters. She was absorbed in the sweet pink baby bundled up in her arms as she rocked and murmured between kisses to her face and tiny hands, still humming snatches of "Mary was a grand old name."

"Don't you worry about anything at all there, you sweet child. You are safe here with us and we'll never, ever let anything happen to you. You have the best Mom and Dad in the whole wide world and a grandma and grandpa and auntie who love you more than anything. Anything in the whole world. Don't you worry about a thing ever, not ever, Mary, honey."

Hank and I sighed and looked at each other. Agnes looked perplexed but I knew exactly what my husband was thinking.

"Mary Honey."

I nodded.

That Christmas was the first one in our new home with our new baby. Mama showed Hank how to get the mason jar and put the candle way down inside of it so that it wouldn't flicker out in the cold winter night air. And all of us traipsed, with the baby on the old wooden sled, down the country lane under a mantle of Christmas stars to leave not one but two lights in the darkness of the December night. One for Mama and Dad's household, and one for Hank and me and Mary Honey. And that's how it was from then on.

And back in our cozy little kitchen we trimmed our first Christmas tree with popcorn strings and dried red berries. Mama gave me my own baby's first Christmas ball from 1935 to hang on my first tree and many thereafter. She also gave me the Dominion Seedhouse structure and she and I were laughing as we hung the new one up that we'd made together.

"Mary Honey 1954."

You had to be a survivor, to be born on October 15, 1954 and flourish. And she was.

Mary turned out to be the number one name of 1954. Who could have ever guessed that? But then it *was* a grand, old name, to be sure.

"That was your grandma, Hannah dear," I whispered to this new baby who was sleeping in my arms. It was almost impossible for me to believe that Mary Honey was a grandmother. I was just getting used to the fact that she was a mother. I felt somehow as if I had overstayed my welcome–as if my life was winding down and down and I was passing on the torch to the ones coming up. The circle of life. It was a fact. Children came and grew and lived their lives and you just had to cherish them as they flew by along the way.

We had certainly cherished Mary Honey. She came into a complete circle of family love. The world is so very different now. I look down at brand new Hannah and I have no idea what is in store for her. As the years go by and technology advances in leaps and bounds it's just anybody's guess what will happen down the road.

It wasn't like that in the fifties. A wife and mother knew exactly what was expected of her. I suppose it would seem very dull and mundane to young girls nowadays, but I remember at that time in my life greeting each day with great joy. I would marvel in the new miracle that was Mary Honey and my love for Hank. She was a very good baby and we enjoyed every second of every day with her. It seemed as if she had been born with a sunny nature. It's funny how such an even-tempered child had been born out of such chaos as had existed on that dark October day.

I saw Mama every day. Either she slipped over through the fields or I pulled the baby across on a sled or wagon, whatever the weather permitted. We baked together and did preserves and lay on the old worn rug playing with the baby, kissing her and laughing into her sweet face and watching with wonder as she crawled and then toddled and then raced across the calendar of our lives.

Aggie loved her, too. She would hurry home hoping to play with her for a while before I had to hightail it back over the fields and home to wait for my Hank. Aggie turned out to be her biggest fan. We'd never really had any very small children around and we were unprepared for the huge quantities of love which Mary Honey left in her wake.

That's what she ended up being called in everyday life quite by accident, really. It just seemed to stick, and the name suited her.

Mama always said that you can't spoil a child by loving them and Mary Honey was certainly living proof of that.

I smiled with nostalgia as I held little Hannah of today. Christmas, I remembered, became exciting and wondrous as Mary Honey grew and participated in the festivities. Mama had that child baking cookies with her from a very early age. Agnes and I laughed as we recalled how we'd had to be very careful with the ingredients and try very hard not to make a mess when we were little. We came in from Christmas shopping one day to find Mama and Mary Honey, at the ripe age of barely two years old, with the kitchen floor almost totally covered in flour and bits of dough on every square inch of the table, not to mention in Mary Honey's fuzzy blonde hair.

"Wow!" Aggie exclaimed. "Hannah and I certainly were never allowed to make a mess like this. We would have been chased around the kitchen with you and your apron flapping behind us."

Mama was indignant.

"I don't ever remember doing that, Aggie. You're exaggerating."

"I'm not, Ma. We had to be so very neat and couldn't have so much as a speck of flour on the floor. Isn't that right, Hannah?"

She appealed to me but I was reluctant to side against Mama, partly because she seemed genuinely perplexed to have no memory of this, but mainly because she was so good with Mary Honey who was obviously enjoying herself to no end.

I hesitated and tried for neutral grounds.

"Is that the recipe that we've always used for shortbread, Mama?"

'Oh, yes. It makes the best cookies to roll out and little miss here does love to roll them out and cut shapes."

Agnes shrugged, reached for a dubious looking angel and popped it into her mouth. Mary Honey was chortling happily as she continued to apply a liberal amount of red and green sprinkles to something which she appeared to be fashioning from some dough remnants.

"One pound of butter

One cup of fruit powder sugar

Four cups of flour. . .."

Agnes recited the recipe as she reached for another cookie.

"That's right, dear. Best shortbread cookies ever. It was my mom's recipe, God rest her soul."

These Christmas memories are very clear to me as I tip my head to look gently and longingly down the expanse of years-of Christmases Past.

Even though Hank and I lived in our own house and had our own lives, we were quite entwined with Mama and Dad and Agnes. Our Christmases were always together. The days and weeks in November and December were spent baking and sewing and preparing.

We played Monopoly in the evenings sometimes when we would settle in front of the fire. Dad always won, of course. He had a good head for figures. But Mama won a lot of the brainteaser games that we played. I have no idea where she got her endless stream of knowledge except that she read a lot and thought that reading was the very best thing that you could do to improve your brain. Mama hadn't gone very far in school–a lot of people from her generation hadn't–but it would have been hard to find someone who could match wits against her in everyday knowledge. And Christmas knowledge was her specialty.

Agnes and I were constantly amazed by her answers to brainteaser questions pertaining to Christmas. Agnes, who was going through school to be a teacher, would accumulate things to ask Mama starting in September and then we would have competitions. I suppose it was a rather crude version of the board game Trivial Pursuit that people play now. Except Agnes seemed to make up the rules as she went along.

"Do you know who wrote *The Grinch Who Stole Christmas?*" Agnes asked as we settled down one cold December evening to play our game. She looked around at us. Mary Honey was sitting up on the couch with Hank looking at a copy of that self same book. It had been a new book this year and Mary Honey was enjoying the sounds of the silly words which the author had strung together. She was just three and sharp as a whip. I thought that we could have turned the book around to check and see who the author was but I knew anyways. I had loved his first book, *And to Think That I Saw It on Mulberry Street*. I loved it for its wackiness and its wild imaginings.

"Dr. Seuss!" I cried out triumphantly.

"You're right, dear." Mama declared and I couldn't help but think that this had been a little too easy. Agnes usually had a trick to her questions. She was mainly trying to outwit Mama. There was simply no challenge at all to outwitting me.

Hank turned the book over and looked at the front cover.

"She is right, Aggie," he declared.

I thought that he didn't have to sound quite so surprised but refrained from mentioning this, basking in the knowledge that I had gotten the correct answer.

"Ah-ha!" Aggie held up her hand and looked at me, though I knew that her question was really directed at Mama. "Ah-ha. Is that his real name?"

"Of course it is," Hank said. "It's written right here on the front cover."

"Do *you* think that's his real name, Mama?"

"Is it worth an extra point?" I inquired. "Because if it's not then I don't see how it matters."

"It's worth a bonus point."

"Oh, you just make up rules as you go along," I grumbled.

"No I don't. It's a legitimate question."

Mama had her head down, ostensibly concentrating on darning Mary Honey's little sweater, but I was sure that she was hiding a grin.

"Well, Mama, anyone? Time's almost up."

"Now we have time limits," I groaned.

"One, two, three–"

"Theodor Geisel. Actually Seuss was his mother's maiden name." Mama looked up from her task at hand, trying but not really succeeding in keeping triumph out of her voice.

Agnes was deflated.

"Mama, how do you know these things? You hardly ever leave the house."

"I read, my child. It's all up here." She tapped her finger against her graying temple and grinned. "And I do love Christmas, you know. I try to read up on it. It's interesting-the different countries and customs and so on."

"It's true," my father sighed deeply. "She sits up and reads long after I go to bed."

"She's always done that."

"I've been reading more lately," Mama said thoughtfully. "I find it quite relaxing, and if I go to bed too early I wake up in the middle of the night and can't get back to sleep."

"Not me. I could go to sleep right now," I declared.

"Of course, dear. You have a young child who keeps you busy. It's different when you're older."

"How old was the Grinch, by the way?" Agnes took the opportunity to interject.

"Fifty-three. Much like myself."

"He was nothing like you, Grandma. The Grinch hated Christmas and the whole Christmas season. And his heart was just too small for himself."

We all laughed at the earnestness of Mary Honey's proclamation in her little girl voice.

"One more question–come on. One more." Aggie was nothing if not persistent.

"One more," Mama agreed, as Hank made noises regarding finding mitts and hats and boots for the short trek across the frozen fields.

Agnes looked down at her sheet of paper with her collection of Christmas questions.

"What do holly and ivy represent in the carol 'The Holly and the Ivy'?"

"I believe," said Mama thoughtfully, pausing with needle in hand. "I believe that holly represents men and ivy represents women. Is that right?"

"Yes, but whom specifically?"

"Well, I suppose Jesus and Mary."

Agnes shook her head and said that wasn't nearly hard enough and that she would get Mama yet. We all just grinned. Mama was so obviously non-competitive and Agnes was just as obviously determined to beat her.

Mama helped Mary Honey with her winter gear and kissed her face which was barely discernible beneath her big wooly scarf. She waved to us at the window in the last glow of the lamp as we traipsed our way home.

"Your Mom sure knows a lot about Christmas, doesn't she?"

I laughed.

"Honestly, Hank I don't know where she gets half of it from. Except that she does love to read."

"And she does love Christmas."

"She sure does. She always has, ever since I can remember. I want to teach Mary Honey to love it like that, too."

I turned to him as the wind whipped my scarf in his direction.

"Don't worry we will. It won't be too hard around your family. Just think, darling, of all the happy Christmases that are waiting for us down the road," said Hank.

I took his hand and squeezed it through the bulk of our mittens.

The fifties went by so quickly. They were good years all in all, I think. The world was breathing a big sigh of relief that peace was prevailing over all. I was busy every day but my life was full and happy.

Those were the years, I explained to new Baby Hannah, when my tree was adorned mainly with homemade ornaments. Mary Honey loved crafts and she spent hours with Mama fashioning decorations for our beloved tree. She made cards too, cutting and pasting and printing her letters painstakingly in red and green to proclaim her unending love and Christmas wishes to all of us. My tree was covered with macaroni shapes painted gold and stockings cut out of red and green felt or just scraps of old flannel with cotton balls glued on them or little sparkles of gold and silver. There was a paper plate Santa with a huge smile and big rosy cheeks and there were several versions of snowflakes that you cut out of a white paper folded and folded over. There was also one wispy delicate Santa which had been manufactured from a milk weed pod and painted inside oh, so carefully. I suspect that Mama had more than a small hand in that one.

I loved my tree and so did Hank. If we were to stop getting any new decorations from then on my tree would have still had a magnificent story of Christmas love and many childish dreams to tell. But of course that was only the bare beginning of my Christmas story, although I have retained quite a number of the more durable ones to make an appearance every year. These things are important. Mama taught me that. These are the things upon which we build the years to come.

Mama never did quite teach me to be such a dab hand at Christmas lore as she was. Mary Honey though, seemed to be following in her grandma's footsteps. Mama read to her a lot and she had a lot of cherished old Christmas books that they pored over together, much to Aggie's chagrin. The years did not lessen my sister's desire to get the better of Mama, and she was infuriated when Mama in her calm, quiet way seemed to remain so well informed.

We would be sitting quietly in the old living room at the farm house and Agnes would begin firing away questions. It was a Christmas tradition by now. I suspected that Mama studied all year any books from the library pertaining to Christmas customs and such but still she had an amazing memory. She always did. And not very often was she stumped. And now my girl was getting into the brain teaser games, as well. She liked to get the answers right, too, of course. But right or wrong it didn't matter. We always knew whose side she was on. Always. It was easy–a no brainer as they say today. She was always on Mama's side.

"Who was Good King Wenceslas?" Aggie's voice was deceptively nonchalant.

"He was in the song about the feast of Stephen," Mary Honey chirped up and began singing the song for Agnes in her young voice.

"When is the Feast of Stephen, smarty pants?" asked Agnes, grinning at her beloved niece.

"I know that, Auntie Agnes. It's Boxing Day."

"Are you sure?"

Mary Honey looked uncertainly at Mama who nodded without looking up from her knitting.

"I am so sure."

"Well you get a point for that, but I still don't have the answer to my question. Who *was* he?"

"He was the guy in the song," Mary Honey explained slowly as if to one who was just a little dim-witted.

"I know that, doll face," Agnes ruffled my daughter's curls and grinned. "I wondered if your grandma knew any more about him, that's all."

"I just bet she does," Mary Honey declared loyally.

Mama looked up and said, "I know that he was a very good man and that he helped the poor and that's why we remember him at Christmas."

"Ye-e-s."

"What else, dear?"

"Do you know who he really was, Mama?"

Mama put down her needles and inclined her head as if giving the matter serious thought but I was quite sure that it was just pretense.

"He was the Duke of Bohemia, dear. And he was a good man, but not everyone thought so. He ended up being murdered by his younger brother. His name escapes me at the moment–the brother's, I mean."

"Score, Grandma." Mary Honey laughed. "Hey, Grandma, why are Christmas trees like bad knitters?"

"I have no idea, my dear."

"They both drop their needles."

Everyone groaned and Mary Honey looked pleased.

"Where did the shape of candy canes come from?" She was on a roll now.

"That's a good question, Mary Honey. Do you know the answer yourself before you ask the others?"

"Yes, I do," Mary Honey said adamantly. "The teacher told us in school last week. Do you know, Auntie Agnes?"

"Yes, I do. You'll have to get up pretty early in the morning to put one over on me."

"Well, what then?" She demanded.

"A shepherd's crook."

"Yay! Auntie Agnes wins," Mary Honey was pleased with her aunt getting the correct answer.

"Good question," Aggie conceded. "What do you want for Christmas anyway, Mary Honey?"

"I want a Barbie doll" she said without hesitation. Barbies had made their debut in 1959 and now, a year later Mary Honey could not stop thinking about them. We did have a Barbie for her that year. I have a black and white photo taken on my old Brownie camera with her clutching it. But that is not all that she received for Christmas that year. Just when Hank and I were beginning to think that Mary Honey might be an only child (because there was no real concrete means of birth control then and you just had to take what you got, so to speak) I found to my immense joy that I was expecting another child.

We thought that it would be a surprise for the new year, but our son was ushered into the world just two days before Christmas of 1960. That was the best Christmas of my whole life. And Mary Honey was thrilled beyond belief. A Barbie doll *and* a baby brother–now we're talking!

The only thing about having a baby before its due date and so close to Christmas to boot was that we didn't have a name for him. Mama had been gluing and sewing with feverish haste at a Christmas ball to commemorate baby boy Moreau's birth but as yet the felt was not cut out to form a name. We were tossing names back and forth between us but nothing seemed to suit the little scrap of humanity that was our new son.

The night before Christmas Eve we were sitting together by the fire pausing for some quiet time before the Christmas rush. I had just fed my sweet boy and Mama had taken him and was rocking him in her worn old chair.

The television was on and it was turned to a music show: Don Messers' *Jubilee*, I think, something from down east, and a young girl started to sing, in a powerful voice, "Oh, Danny Boy." It was quite beautiful. Not Christmasy to be sure but very touching. After the music had ended I could hear Mama softly singing to my little lad as she gently rocked him. And of course she was singing "Oh Danny Boy."

Hank and I looked at each other and laughed softly.

"Is this going to happen every time we have a baby?" Hank asked.

"I don't know." I laughed. "We've only had two."

"What are you talking about, Daddy?" Mary Honey was puzzled.

"Oh, it's just that your grandma seems to sing our babies into their names, that's all."

"Like now?"

"Yes, dear."

"Does that mean that the baby will be named Oh Danny Boy?"

Hank and I looked at each other and nodded.

Mary Honey smiled approvingly. "I like it," she declared.

She went over to her grandma who stopped her rocking and put her free arm around my daughter. Then she switched her song to "Mary Was a Grand Old Name." Mary Honey was familiar with this song, of course. It wouldn't be long, I was sure, until she'd be crooning out "Danny Boy" as well.

That night while the whole rest of the world slept Mama sat up just a little longer than usual and cut out the appropriate letters from the waiting felt to glue on the ball that was already prepared for Christmas, just in case. It would be shining from the tree in the morning.

"Danny's first Christmas 1960."

"Oh Danny Boy, Oh Danny Boy, I love you so."

Those words said it all. I did love him so, my little boy baby, my little sunshine, my Danny Boy. He was sweet and happy and gurgly. He smiled early and laughed early and when he laughed he sort of bubbled over with joy. It was great. You absolutely forget how joyful it is to have a baby take up residence in your house. You forget how much work it is to be sure. This was before disposable diapers and microwaves and all of the conveniences that we take for granted nowadays. But somehow life was simpler.

I sighed, as I half-thought, half-whispered this to new baby Hannah. I sounded like an old fuddy duddy who kept looking to the past and always thought that the years which had been were infinitely better than the present ones. Sometimes it was hard not to feel like that. Life seemed so much slower then, somehow. We were always busy but we were always together–working together. The years slipped away and they were composed of days upon days of happy hours spent in our home and hearth. I sighed again. God alone knew what was in store for this wee mite of the modern world.

Mary Honey was in absolute heaven to have a baby brother. She toted him around and rocked him and sang to him in her sweet little off-key six-year-old voice. Between her and Mama it's a wonder I ever got to hold my new bundle. It was hard to conceive of a child being more loved than Daniel Henry Moreau.

The Cold War was raging in the big world outside of our Ontario farm. In August of 1961 the Berlin wall went up, cutting Germany in two with its blocks of concrete, and many young men in America were killed at an alarming rate in the senseless slaughter of Viet Nam. But we were largely untouched by all of this. We knew about it, of course, and followed the world events closely, but it was very far from our everyday lives.

Mary Honey was in school now and every morning I would walk with Danny down the long, dusty lane to wait for the bus to come bustling along in the early morning light. Most of the mornings Mama was there, too, so that she could give Mary Honey a hug and kiss and wave as she climbed aboard the bus. Then she would usually walk back with Danny and me and we'd have a cup of tea together (because there was always time for a cup of tea.) We often pooled our household chores. We would bake together or do preserves and canning and pickling. On the farm there is always something that needs to be put up, the fruit and the vegetables. We even tried our hand at making wine from dandelions with questionable results. We were never idle but I remember the hours as being happy, contented ones. I wonder if the past is always like that. Perhaps you only remember the happy memories and sift out the unpleasant ones. This could well be true; however, when I look back on those days, they always seem golden in colour and full of joy.

Agnes was in Teachers' College by now. Those were the days when teachers' college only constituted one year. So Agnes was very busy, which meant that Mama was able to spend a lot of time with me. I was very blessed.

This didn't stop Aggie from formulating Christmas trivia questions for our mother, though.

Of course Mama didn't know every answer but she continued to astound us with the knowledge that she did possess.

"I have to be noted for something," She'd say modestly when we would exclaim at her answers. Well, Mary Honey and I would exclaim. Agnes just continued to try to ensnare her.

"Who invented the Christmas card?"

"Sir Henry Cole."

"Ah ha! How do you even know that?"

"What do you mean 'ah ha'?" I asked. "Is that right or not?"

"I mean, why do you know that?"

"Why not, dear?" Mama asked reasonably. This caused Dad and Mary Honey to chuckle.

Mary Honey always said that she was going to learn Christmas facts too so that she could help Mama as she got older. I've said it before and I'll say it again–there was never any question of sides, not ever. Mary Honey was unfailingly on Mama's side.

"She doesn't need any help," grumped Agnes.

Mama was modestly quiet with her needle and thread.

"Who is credited with setting up the first nativity scene?"

Mama remained silent as she darned the heel of Dad's sock and Agnes called out triumphantly, "Don't know?"

"Oh, sorry, dear." She bit the thread and surveyed the finished product critically.

'It was Francis of Assisi, of course."

"Of course." Agnes' tone was sarcastic but Mama chose to misunderstand which was a fairly standard way to deal with my sister. I didn't miss the twinkle in Mom's eye, though. I knew that she loved to put one over on Agnes.

"I always did love St Francis," she went on. "He was so good to the animals–a very human saint, I've always thought."

"How long is the Christmas Yule log supposed to burn?" Agnes demanded, totally ignoring and probably not caring about the virtues of the good St Francis.

"For the twelve days of Christmas," Mary Honey piped up in her young voice.

"That is right, dear." Mama said proudly.

"You two are as bad as each other," Agnes complained.

"Or as good as each other," Hank suggested. "Depends on how you look at it."

"I suppose."

"You just have to believe in Christmas, like Grandma and I, right, Mom?"

"Right. That's why we always leave a light on at the end of the lane. Because we believe in Christmas. Aunt Agnes is just trying to win the game, that's all."

Agnes smiled ruefully.

"It's not even a game" Agnes said. "I just try to stump your Grandma but I think that she keeps busy all year boning up on Christmas facts."

"She could be doing a lot worse things," my father interjected. He, too, was loyal.

"I know, Dad."

"Anyways wait until you see the ornament that Grandma and I made for the tree this year. Can I hang it up now, Grandma?"

"You go get it, Mary Honey."

As Mary Honey leapt up the stairs to retrieve the ornament from its hiding place in her room, Mama turned to me and explained in an undertone that she thought it might be a little too big for the Christmas tree but she didn't want to dampen the child's spirit.

"Oh I'm sure it will be fine, Mama," I reassured her as I critiqued the tall pine with its homemade adornments including painted pine cones, popcorn garlands and sugared fruit slices.

Mary Honey came downstairs at a slower pace and shyly handed me a piece of paper with red and green construction papered balls decorating the outside. I could see that Mama had helped but I could also see that Mary Honey had labored over it to make the letters small and even and legible. It had a silver hook made of aluminum foil for easy hanging. I smiled as I read:

"Oh Danny boy, the pipes, the pipes are calling
From glen to glen, and down the mountain side
The summer's gone and all the flowers are dying
'Tis you,'tis you must go and I must bide.
But come ye back when summer's in the meadow
Or when the valley's hushed and white with snow

'Tis I'll be here in sunshine or in shadow
Oh Danny boy, oh Danny boy, I love you so."

I turned it over. The second verse was written out just as painstakingly on the back but we only ever sang the first verse to our little man.

"It is so beautiful, my darling." I hugged my girl. I was glad that she loved Christmas as we did.

"Well done, love," agreed Hank. "Hang it on the tree."

"Where shall I hang it? It's kind of big."

"It's fine," Agnes pronounced. "Here, Mary Honey, hang it over here beside Danny's first Christmas. It can tell his story."

"He doesn't have a very long story. He's just barely one"

"I know but he will. There. It looks good there."

And Mary Honey had to agree that it did.

She danced over and picked up her brother who was looking at the tree in a milk stupor.

"That is for you. See. That's the song that Mom and Grandma and I sing to you. Right up there on the tree."

Danny looked up and clapped his hands with glee, more I'm sure from the excitement and the pretty lights than anything. It didn't matter, though. It made his sister laugh.

I looked across the room and caught Hank's eye.

"We have happy children." I declared.

He nodded his head.

"We do at that."

The '60s were booming, for sure. Things were changing so quickly. One of the big changes for Canada was the opening of the Trans-Canada Highway.

On Sept. 3, 1962, Prime Minister John Diefenbaker stood at one end of it in British Columbia and declared it officially open. It was possible to drive from St John's, Newfoundland to Victoria, Vancouver Island on Canadian roads. It was a dream come true for Canadians.

Hank and I used to talk about how some day we would drive the whole length of our fair country. We would take the children and travel like nomads and see all of the provinces-the beauty of the Maritimes, the splendor and vast outlying of our own province, the everlasting prairies with their miles and miles of glorious farmland, and of course, the majesty of the Rockies. It was a pipe dream but sometimes that's a good thing to have.

Someday, we'd tell each other, we'll just get in the car and explore and see what there is to see. It's nice to have a "someday" dream.

We never actually got too far at all. Gas, after all, was 30 cents a gallon and bread was ten cents a loaf and things were going up all of the time. We had to be careful. We had two children to raise and Hank and I were of one mind regarding this. Our kids were the mainstay and cornerstone of our existence.

It was the '60s, though. Many young folk were taking off with little more than backpacks and their thumbs to explore the miles and miles that stretched out on the new expanse of the Trans-Canada Highway.

And on December 15th, 1964 (just in time to make it as an ornament on our family Christmas tree, much to Mama's glee) Canada gave birth to a brand new flag.

The Canadian flag, previously, had always been a little difficult to pin down. I remember Agnes and me trying to reproduce it as children in school. It just wasn't easy. It was a combination of the Union Jack and the Canadian Red Ensign. If anyone remembers it I am quite sure that he or she will agree-it was complicated.

I loved the new flag. I was and always have been very patriotic. I loved the idea of our flag in its' distinct red and white and its' beautiful maple leaf. I felt that it was uniquely Canadian. I helped

Mary Honey trace it over and over so that we could admire it.

Prime Minister Lester Pearson was the man who gave us our new flag and I loved him for it. He was born just around Toronto and I felt that he was on our side. He took a lot of flak at the time but over the years the Maple Leaf has become a uniquely Canadian symbol.

The red and white replica of our new flag which adorned our tree that year was a sight to behold. After all, my mama had ten whole days to produce such a creation. This from a woman who had fashioned an outstanding "Danny's first Christmas" ornament in only one night. She was not going to let an important year like 1964 go by without recognition. A new Canadian flag was a momentous occasion. Mama had always loved the maple leaf and she deeply approved of this new choice.

If I close my eyes right this very moment I can hear Mama singing

"The maple leaf–our emblem dear
The maple leaf forever
God save our Queen and heaven bless
The Maple Leaf forever."

As a loyal Canadian, through and through, I cannot omit the Centennial Year as I quietly murmur the history of my tree to an unsuspecting Hannah. She was so silent and sweet and I had hours and hours to think of all the significant events portrayed on those branches. I smiled to myself as I thought of the hype and excitement that 1967 had caused all over our country: one hundred years since the signing of Confederation in Prince Edward Island. Canadians as a rule were not as openly patriotic as our neighbours the Americans, but 1967 was an exception to that rule.

The ornament which represented that "very good year" to quote Pierre Burton [as a matter of fact, he referred to it as the last good year] was another one which had been manufactured by Mary Honey and Mama. It was the logo of Canada's centennial celebrations in the shape of a maple leaf fashioned out of a series of triangles. It was a common enough sight during that year and all of the triangles were different colours: the top one was purple, the right ones were green and red, the ones on the left pink and yellow with blue and orange and varying shades in between comprising the middle triangles. On the back was written in large black numbers "1967."

I smiled as I remembered back to that good year. Mary Honey had been twelve and Danny seven.

They were involved in everything they could be. Celebrations were held throughout the nation, whether large scale or just community events, as we had. The school which the kids attended was Alloa Public and it was a real country school. Most of the kids were farm kids or at least rural. All of them went on buses.

Our farm was between Norval which was quite small and the larger town of Georgetown, which at that time was not too much bigger. The Credit River ran through Norval and Lucy Maud Montgomery, that great Canadian author had lived there, writing several of her books during this time. Other than that we had no real claim to fame. But we were as proud as any other community. We had celebrations and fireworks and even a play at the school where the kids dressed up as pioneers and tried to portray the life of our forefathers.

Pierre Burton, perhaps, was right. It was a very good year. The nation had begun to feel more nationalistic than ever with a generation raised in a country fully detached from Britain. The new Canadian flag was a symbol and a catalyst for this. Hank bought a huge one at the Norval General Store and we proudly raised it on July 1st to wave brightly on the hill beside our house where there was always a wind, even on the hottest of days.

The Canadian economy was at its post war peak and levels of prosperity were at their best ever. Medicare and Canada Pension Plan were coming on line, and the quality of life was finally improving for Canadians.

And on May 2nd the Toronto Maple Leafs won its fourth Stanley

Cup in six years by defeating its arch rival the Montreal Canadians. It was their last Stanley Cup to date, but that doesn't matter. It was a great night. Dad and Hank, both of whom rarely drank, were having beer and whooping uproariously as the game progressed. Hank was just carried away I think but Dad was an avid Leafs fan till the day he died. He never stopped believing in them, which is more than can be said for a lot of Canadians. He believed that if you were on their side, then you were there whether they were winning or losing. That just about sums up my dad in a nutshell. And if he was on your side, you knew he would never waver. Of course, that included all of his family. How lucky we were!

One of my fondest memories of that very good year is the end of school concert, which was put on by Mary Honey's class on a hot June evening. The teacher was young and very enthusiastic and had put an amazing amount of effort into teaching her young students both the English and the French lyrics of the Centennial Song. It was written by Bobby Gimby to celebrate Canada's centennial and Expo '67. She had them all aligned on the little stage in the auditorium, clothed in red and white, and conducted them proudly as they sang, beaming:

CA-NA-DA
[One little two little three Canadians]
We love thee
{Now we are twenty million}
CA-NA-DA
[Four little five little six little Provinces]
Proud and free
[Now we are ten and the Territories sea to sea]

North south east west
There'll be happy times
Church bells will ring, ring, ring

It's the hundredth anniversary of Confederation
Everybody sing together!

CA-NA-DA
[Un petit, deux petit, trios Canadiens]
Notre pays
[Maintenant, nous sommes vingt million]
CA-NA-DA

The teacher gestured for all of the families to join in and we all sang the English version together. Very few, if any of us country folk would know any French but we were all proud of the children singing their hearts out. They sang the second chorus with enthusiasm;

Rah! Vive le Canada!
Three cheers Hip, Hip Hooray!
Le centenaire,
That's the order of the day
Frere Jacques Frere Jacques
Merrily we roll along
Together all the way.
[Quatre petites, cinq petites, six petites provinces]
Longue vie
[Et nous sommes dix plus les Territoires, Longue vie]
Nord, sud, est, oust
Ding, dong, ding
Alons Canadiens, tres unis,
Le centenaire de la
Confederation
Les enfants du pays, ensemble!

I can still remember the heat and humidity emitting from the old auditorium that evening. I remember some people were becoming restless and impatient, but I thought it was a night to be treasured. Which indeed it was.

Mama and Dad were there, and Agnes of course as she was a teacher. All of the neighbours were there including our minister and Dr Morrison, our local GP, watching his grandson with pride.

To end the celebrations and indeed the school year, everyone was invited to sing the Centennial provincial song which had also become very popular. You could hear snatches of it anywhere that year. It was a catchy tune. Danny loved it and sung along loudly with probably more enthusiasm than skill, but it mattered not. If I close my eyes, as I rock my little darling, I can visualize Danny singing in his happy young voice and Mama with her arm around him singing as well and beaming at him, glad to be included in the celebrations. Dad didn't really sing but my Hank did and I did and Mary Honey, who remained up on the stage, sure did. It was uproarious.

"Give us a place to stand
And a place to grow
We call this land
Ontario
A place to live
For you and me
With hopes as high
As the tallest tree
Give us a land of lakes
And a land of snow
And we will build
Ontario
A place to stand, a place to grow
Ontari-ari-ari-o
From Western hills,
To northern shores
To Niagara Falls

Where the waters roar
Give us a land of peace
Where the free winds blow
And we will build
Ontario
A place to stand, a place to grow
Ontari-ari-ari-o!"

I looked at the Centennial logo hanging on my tree and I was glad that I could still remember that year, those songs and celebrations–that hot, laughter-filled night when our Canadian world was only one hundred years old.

I'll grant you one thing, Pierre–it *was* a very good year. Yes indeed.

The world was so very different then. It is hard to even imagine how life was -even for me, who lived through those years. I know that there are so many things that are better now–more convenient for sure, and easier. But sometimes, I long with all my heart for those old days which seem so remote now. I can look back and think of them fondly. They exist in a soft haze of peace–of busy, happy days spent with Mama in the kitchen and the kids playing and laughing. Even as I think this I know that it wasn't as idyllic as I'm recalling it. I know that the kids often fought and I was tired and disgruntled at times. But I always felt centered and secure. I knew what I was meant to do and I got pleasure out of doing it. Mama kept us all so grounded.

The only telephone accessible to you was the one that your whole household used, and it was connected with a cord. If you lived in the country, then you were on a party line and only a certain ring signified that the call was for your specific household. And if the neighbors were nosy [as country folk have a tendency to be] then you could not be absolutely certain that your conversation would not be the subject of someone else's dinner small talk. You weren't allowed to talk on it for very long because it was considered rude and you simply didn't answer it during supper time [also rude].

School was different as well. The teacher was the boss and if you didn't do what you were told you were "taught to the tune of the hickory stick." In other words, you got the strap. And that was just a given. The teachers were right and any punishment they meted out was considered fair and just.

These were the years of the Cold War and the Viet Nam War when countless numbers of young Americans lost their lives overseas. These were the years of "love-ins" and "women's lib." LSD and other drugs were rampant, or so it would seem. Some of our neighbours found marijuana plants among the thick of their corn one summer but we never did. Hank and I read about things and tried to keep up to date but our life was pretty straightforward. We were busy all of the time but there was always time for family. That is what I remember the most. That is what makes my heart long for the "good old days."

I think that really the best years and the best Christmases were not the really remarkable ones when big events happened. I have marked them on my tree and I want to give them every credit possible. But some of the most beloved to my heart are the ones that just slipped by year after year–the ones when the kids were at home and we were always together. Life was just ordinary and that was okay. It is as we age that we realize they are the ordinary days that shape our lives. The little Christmas ways that repeat themselves year after year until they become our yuletide traditions.

The fruitcake was such a tradition. Agnes and I always laughed and joked with each other as we made fruitcake because the truth and the whole truth was that neither one of us cared for it, not in the least. The children never really acquired a taste for it and Hank would have a piece because he was a polite soul. I don't think that I ever really saw Mama or Dad eat more than a little piece themselves.

This begged the question that Agnes and I always asked each other in private every Christmas: "Does anybody really like fruitcake?" We chuckled over this but we never actually found an answer. That was another thing about those days–people seemed more able to leave well enough alone.

Whatever the answer to that oft-asked question, the reality was that every blessed year in November we started the fruitcake process.

We had all of our nuts and figs ready. The walnuts grew on the old tree at the back of the farm and the kids and I would gather them in the fall and dry them out in the barn. When they were old and dry we would pound them with a hammer and get the walnuts out for Mama's fruitcake. We also had candied fruit and peel which was preserved fruit that had been dipped several times in concentrated sugar syrup.

The cake had to be made at least three to four weeks before Christmas so that it could be brushed with alcohol several times and the flavors could mingle and age together.

If anyone out there really does like fruitcake–because Agnes and I are sure someone does–I am enclosing this old recipe of Mama's. And because how could you really write a Christmas book without a fruitcake recipe? Maybe a modern one, but not an old fashioned one, surely not.

Mama's Christmas Cake

1 cup unsalted butter
½ cup dark brown sugar
½ cup light brown sugar
3 large eggs
3 tablespoons brandy [plus extra for brushing the cake]
Juice and zest of one orange
Zest of one lemon
¾ cup ground almonds

1 cup pecans, chopped
1 cup walnuts, chopped
1 and ½ lbs. of an assortment of dried fruits which could include dried apricots, figs of prunes, candied and chopped mixed peel and glace cherries–these should all be chopped into bite-size pieces
¾ of a pound of raisins and currants
2 cups flour
1 teaspoon baking powder
Dash of salt

Grease the bottom of a spring form pan with a removable bottom. Line the bottom with buttered parchment paper. Also line the sides of the pan with a strip of buttered parchment paper that extends above the pan. Preheat the oven to 325 degrees.

In the bowl beat the butter and the sugars together until they are light and fluffy. Add eggs, one at a time, beating well after each addition. Scrape bowl, as needed. Add the brandy, juice, and the zest of the lemon and juice and zest of the orange. Then fold in the ground almonds, chopped nuts and all the dried and candied fruits. In a separate bowl whisk together the flour, salt and baking powder and fold this into the cake batter.

Scrape the batter into the prepared pan and place the spring form pan on a larger baking sheet. Bake in the oven for one hour. Reduce the oven temperature to 300 degrees and continue to bake for another hour and a half or until a large skewer inserted into the center of the cake comes out clean with only a few moist crumbs. Remove from the oven and place it on a wire rack to cool completely. With a skewer poke holes in the top surface of the cake and brush with a little brandy.

Wrap the cake thoroughly in a plastic wrap and aluminum foil and place in a cake tin. Brush the cake periodically [once or twice a week] with brandy until Christmas.

Mama had a fruit cellar downstairs and we would store the cake there and religiously brush it so that it would be well lubricated for Christmas.

I can still remember the smell of that cake while it cooked away in the kitchen and we peered at it as we busied ourselves with other baking and tasks. That is a smell which truly belongs to the past, as neither Agnes nor I has kept up that particular tradition.

And if the subject comes up, or if we are in the presence of a piece of fruitcake, we can be transported right back to our younger selves and dissolve into giggles as we whisper to each other:

"*Does* anybody really like fruitcake?"

Well, do they?

I wish I knew.

Do you?

Danny was about ten years old when I first noticed that things weren't quite right with Mama. I desperately tried to ignore this and succeeded for a little while. However, reality has a way of crashing down around us no matter how hard we try to keep it away.

We were such a happy family. I know that when people look back at their younger years they tend to see everything in a wholesome light and forget the bad parts. Truly, though, I don't remember anything except love and happiness for the first thirty five years of my life. It sounds corny now. It is quite fashionable to have had a difficult childhood and all kinds of problems, but I didn't know that then and I was rarely unhappy. A lot of it was due to Mama and her positive approach to our lives and family. We made the most of each day and enjoyed life fully. Not to say that we didn't work hard. That goes hand-in-hand with farming life. But it was a good life too.

Aggie came to see me one day on her way home from her school teaching job in Norval. It was getting on in the year and she blustered in with a shudder and a gust of cold air that felt suspiciously like approaching winter.

She sat down at my kitchen table, accepting a cup of tea and a chocolate chip cookie and announced solemnly,

"We have to talk."

"Why?" My response was wary.

"It's Mama."

I shut my eyes and sighed deeply. Then I opened them and looked into my sister's serious blue eyes. They were full of worry and concern. Denial was a luxury which Agnes had never allowed herself.

"I know." My voice came out in a whisper–a resigned whisper.

"Hannah, something's wrong."

"I know," I repeated sadly.

Aggie looked relieved. I'm sure that she was prepared for my usual response that everything was fine, just fine.

"Some days she's okay, you know," I said. Somehow I felt disloyal to Mama talking about her like this when she wasn't even present to defend herself.

"You're right, she is. But then there are days when she is really bad, Hannah. I think there's something neurologically wrong with her at times." Aggie spoke just a little loftily. Every once in a while she liked to remind me ever so subtly that she was, after all, a school teacher and every one knows how knowledgeable teachers are. Today I didn't care.

"Have you talked to Dad?"

"Oh, Hannah you know what he's like. He's so private and he wouldn't want to admit that there was anything wrong. I mean he thinks the world of her. But denial never helps." She said this last quite sternly. I'm sure it was directed squarely at me.

"The other day I was over there and she seemed really confused. Dad tried to cover for her but she was so confused that she wasn't even aware of it. She didn't think anything was wrong. She couldn't remember my name even. Dad had to prompt her. It was so weird, Hannah. And then by the time we'd finished our tea she was right as rain. If I didn't know Mama so well I'd swear that she was faking."

"I know that she's not sleeping properly. She did tell me that one day. She said that it's not unusual for her to be awake half the night."

"Well, she's right about that." Agnes said. "She never did need all that much sleep. Remember how she'd always stay up later than all of us?" Suddenly her eyes glistened with tears. "I always thought she stayed up half the damned night studying Christmas trivia so she could beat me and Mary Honey. I'm sure she boned up on it all year so she could look good in December."

I reached over and patted her hand gently.

"You're right, Aggie, she always did stay up later than the rest of the house. I think that was probably the only alone time she got regularly. But I think she slept when she went to bed. I don't ever remember her complaining that she couldn't sleep. And I don't remember her being up through the night."

"I don't even know if that has anything to do with anything. Except maybe she's getting confused from sleep deprivation. That can do funny things to people. Maybe that's the whole problem. Maybe she just needs a damned sleeping pill or something."

Agnes was warming to this theme now, and I had to smile.

"Well, I sure hope so. It would be nice if it could be solved that easily. But I don't know. Have you noticed her walk, Aggie? She walks so stiffly–almost like a shuffle at times. Only at times though. Sometimes she's fine."

"I have noticed that. But as you say, it comes and goes, so what the hell does that mean?"

"It means we have to get her to a doctor, I guess," I said most reluctantly.

Aggie sighed.

"That's not going to be easy. Dad is so stubborn. He doesn't want there to be anything wrong so ergo there isn't anything wrong. You know how his mind works."

I nodded. Oh, yes I knew. I understood that kind of logic.

"Unless one of us goes and talks to Dr. Morrison. My God, she's only seventy. Surely there's something that can be done. They have pills for everything nowadays."

"One of us?"

"Well you know–you, Hannah dear."

"Me?"

"Yes, you know him better what with the kids and all. And I am quite busy teaching."

I bit my tongue to refrain from saying that I wasn't exactly sitting around on my derriere.

We parted with the agreement that I would talk to Dr. Morrison if Agnes had no luck with our dad.

And I was left with a chill in the bottom of my heart which took up residence there for a long, long time.

This all happened in the early 1970's. This was when the family doctor treated the whole family and knew everyone inside and out. Dr. Morrison was like that. He'd delivered me and my children. We saw him at church and at the local shops and he had always liked and respected my mother. He had no qualms about discussing my mom with me, conceding that as family I had a right to know. There were no privacy acts in our small village at that time. If you were family, that was enough.

He listened solemnly to my concerns, shaking his head sadly. When I had finished my tale of the interrupted sleep, the stiff, jerky gait and the periods of confusion he crossed his arms across his broad chest and sighed deeply.

"I know, Hannah. I know this is happening and it makes me most unhappy."

Oh, great, I thought. *You're unhappy.*

"She is a fine woman–one of the finest I've ever known. And I've known her a long time. I delivered you." He smiled kindly. "And all of these years I've known all of you. You're a great bunch."

I smiled sadly at him because, not being a complete idiot, I could tell that his news was not going to be good. He was leading me gently to something quite unpleasant.

He is probably getting close to Mama's age himself, I thought. He had seemed old when I was a child and he didn't look much different now. His hair was grayer and the lines on his face were more pronounced but other than that he looked the same. He was a comforting sort of man–gruff at times but certainly not unkind. He seemed to be picking his words with care today which gave me cause for concern-more concern than I already had.

"I don't know if you know this or not, Hannah–I'm guessing you don't by the sound of it–but your dad was by with your mom about this very problem. I probably shouldn't be telling you this but I think that you and Agnes know when to hold your tongues. I think we've all known each other long enough for that."

I nodded silently. Dread was filling my heart. If Dad was worried, the situation was bad indeed. I don't remember my father ever going to the doctor except once when he had kidney stones and he thought that he was going to die anyways so it didn't matter.

Dr. Morrison smiled.

"I know what you're thinking. I was pretty surprised to see him, too. Farmers as a rule have to be just about dead before they darken the door of a doctor's office."

I laughed in rueful agreement.

"Your mom was pretty good the day she was in and I think your dad felt a little foolish. It's like he made this monumentous decision to come in and then everything appears to be okay. Your dad is a good man, though. He didn't talk about your mother as if she wasn't in the room and he didn't try to hide his concerns. As I say, she was good that day and she was able to verbalize concerns of her own."

"Really?"

Agnes and I had been so nervous about mentioning anything disturbing to our parents that we had clearly underestimated their ability to face life head on.

"She's a fine woman, Hannah," Dr. Morrison repeated. "And a very realistic one. She was able to tell me things that she has noticed herself. She is also aware that she has good days and ones that aren't so good.'

"What has she noticed herself?" My tone sounded a little sharp to my ears and I tried to soften it with a smile. "I have to report to Agnes, the schoolteacher, you know."

Dr. Morrison chuckled.

"I will try to be concise. She has noticed that her depth perception is off at times. And that her movements are quite stiff and shuffling at times, too. Only at times though. Also sometimes she can't remember things."

"Surely we all have that problem from time to time," I suggested ruefully.

"Yes of course. But not like this. For instance she will be totally unable to think of things which have been familiar to her for years. And she's not sleeping. Your father says that some nights she's up for hours and hours roaming around."

"Agnes and I wondered if this could all be caused from lack of sleep-like sleep deprivation."

"Unfortunately in this case the insomnia is a symptom, not a cause."

"How can you be so sure?"

"Well, I can't my dear. But I think that combined with the shuffling gait and the periods of confusion and hallucinations-"

"Hallucinations??"

"Yes, Hannah. Your mom has experienced them only a couple of times but she was aware of them and they frightened her."

I groaned.

"Why hasn't she told us? Why hasn't she talked to Agnes and me?"

"She is trying to protect you, of course. As you, yourself would protect your children if need be. And bear in mind that she is not like this all the time. Sometimes she's perfectly fine."

"I know that. I can see that. But what is the matter? Can we fix it? Do you know?"

"I don't know one hundred per cent, Hannah, but I am making an educated guess that your mom has 'Lewy Body Dementia.'"

I sighed. That just didn't sound good at all. I looked up into his weary brown eyes which had been the bearer of too much bad news for one man. I closed my own tightly. I thought if I kept them closed that perhaps I could ward off bad news by retreating into myself, like a child.

But of course, I opened them again. I took a deep breath and looked into his careworn face.

"Ready?"

I nodded earnestly. I was not going to fall apart. If Mama and Dad could come into this office and cope with bad news then, by God I could too.

"In the early 1900s a scientist called Friederich Lewy was researching Parkinson's disease and he discovered that abnormal protein deposits in the brain can disrupt its normal functioning. These Lewy body proteins can deplete some of the neurotransmitters and cause symptoms such as your mom has–the unsteady gait and the shuffling walk, which are also characteristic of Parkinsons. The brain chemical acetylcholine is depleted because of all of these deposits and that causes disruption of perception, thinking and behavior."

I'm sure that was a good explanation but it meant absolutely the square root of zero to me. The only question that I really wanted to ask stuck on my lips which were suddenly so dry that I was unable to swallow.

"Is there any cure?" I asked in a brand new croaky voice which was not my own.

"No. It is a progressive disease but it's anybody's guess how quickly or slowly it will advance. She may go along like this for years and be not too bad. It's hard to say."

"Should we get a second opinion?"

"Of course that's always an option. I did suggest to your parents that they may want to do just that but they declined. It is a fairly classic presentation."

"Are you sure there's no cure?" I asked, trying to keep the desperate note out of my voice.

"No cure." His tone was sad. "There are some drugs that may or may not help but again your folks declined. They did however accept a prescription for Quinine to help with restless legs at bedtime. I hope that eases the insomnia in turn. It is apparently a very upsetting syndrome. You can imagine if your legs were going haywire on top of everything else."

"She's too young. She's always been so healthy. I don't remember her even having a cold."

"She *is* young. Seventy is young indeed and it's getting younger all the time as we discover new remedies and cures for diseases. But actually anyone from fifty to eighty-five can develop Lewy Body Dementia."

I shuddered.

"Will I get it?"

"I don't know, Hannah. No one does. But you just keep on going and be brave. Just look after those two beautiful children of yours. And give your mom lots of love. She needs it."

"I always do. I just can't believe it, you know. Why she can remember things that no one else in the world would know. She knows this entire repertoire of Christmas trivia. You can't stump her even if you tried. Aggie says that she studies up all year on Christmas facts."

"That's great. The best thing that you can do for your brain is to use it. Your dad actually mentioned the Christmas trivia game. He says she is quite the expert."

"She sure is."

"Keep encouraging her with that if she likes that. And keep your chin up."

He stood up to shake my hand. I forgot how tall he was. I looked up into his craggy old face–the first face that I'd seen on the first day of my life–and I could feel tears falling down my cheeks. I dashed them away and thanked him for his honesty.

"Keep your chin up." He repeated.

"Christmas 2010

Ontario seat belt law celebrates thirty-five years on January 1st 2011. Ontario was the first province to enforce the seat belt laws, and we have been saving many lives because of it."

– Newspaper quote

Thirty-five years! Now that's a lot of water under the bridge. Thirty-five years, indeed. These thoughts would take me back to Christmas 1975 if I let them. Not very often I do. But now I snuggled Hannah's soft warm body close to mine, kissed her sweet baby face and I succumbed.

Slowly, one by one, I let them come to me-the thoughts, the memories, the year that was to shape all of the others to come, my whole life really.

Here's the thing. You can spend hours and hours of your life warning your growing children against the dangers on the road lurking at every turn. You can warn them about safety and speeding and how you should never, ever drink and drive. Nor should you ever get in the car with anyone who had been drinking or smoking dope. You could always call home for a ride any time of the day or night. No one was going to be annoyed at you if you found yourself in a sticky situation. Danny was just barely fifteen years old but I had drilled all of this into his head since he first became a teenager. I had done the same with Mary Honey, of course. She was always a very sensible girl and a good example for Danny. Hank and I kept telling them over and over again the lessons and warnings which all parents give to their children. It almost gives you a false sense of security. You felt that if you said it enough, that it would become an automatic response inside of their minds. That if you told them to "be careful" as they left on a snowy night that they would be so much more careful and thus safer than if you had never uttered those words. Perhaps it just made me feel better. Nonetheless, I lectured whenever I saw the opportunity.

Perhaps I should have been lecturing the other guy.

Dad used to always say that about the rest of the traffic on the road when we would give him our unfailing word that we would be "fine."

"You may be fine," he always said, "but the other guy might be nuts." Or drunk. Or stoned. When I look back down the long corridor which has been my life I know for a fact that Saturday, Dec. 20th, 1975, was the last day of my life when I was completely happy. I have learned a certain degree of happiness since then and have managed quite well with it. I have survived. But never have I had the absolute joy in my soul that I was fortunate enough to have had in all of the days preceding that Saturday evening. The sad thing is that you don't know it–you don't know it until it is taken from you.

I've thought about it so many times-over and over in my head. What if? What if? Senseless, of course, just like all of the what ifs in the world.

Even now I can go over the events of that day perfectly. I just don't know where I should have stopped them if I could have. I will never, ever know.

It was an ordinary day, God bless it. For I have learned since then that the ordinary days are by far the very best. The days that slip by with everyday pleasures and routines. The days of comfort and home life. The days when nothing catastrophic happens and the late afternoon pulls into the night like an old familiar friend.

We'd eaten together as we often did with Mama and Dad. This Saturday they'd come over to our home, and Mama was having a particularly good day. Agnes had joined us, too. Everyone had been in good spirits and we lingered over our after-dinner tea cups, enjoying the pleasure of each other's company. Mary Honey was going to a girlfriend's to study in Brampton, and Danny was going to a hockey game in Georgetown with the neighbors. We watched as their respective rides came to pick them up and sat a little while longer, just chatting and gossiping a little in the old way. I missed it. Mama was not always oriented enough to get much in the way of gossip from her, so I enjoyed it when she seemed to be engaged enough to participate.

Agnes was talking about Christmas [gently, not like in the old days when she would ride my mother about her Christmas tidbits], and also gently, asking Mama a few questions.

"Who was the guy who made Rudolph the Red nosed Reindeer popular, Mom?"

"Why, Gene Autry, dear," was the confident reply.

Dad looked so pleased that it made my heart ache. I knew that deep down, my father was basic and simple and true and he hoped and prayed that if he loved my mom enough that just perhaps she would get better. And what better time than at Christmas? It was quite clear how sharp she still was with her Christmas facts–sometimes.

"What's another name for 'O come all ye faithful'?"

Dad looked warningly at Agnes as if silently entreating her not to tax Mama too much, but Aggie shook her head defiantly. Perhaps I was not the only one in denial about a certain Mr. Lewybody.

"*Adeste Fideles*," Mama pronounced triumphantly and Dad grinned.

The news was on a little later as we lingered into the evening, enjoying the peace and togetherness and anticipating Christmas, which was almost upon us. Dad overheard the name "Patty Hearst" and that was enough to get discussion going for a while–particularly between Dad and Agnes. Hank and I were really on the fence about the case against her, and Mama was not thinking that way these days. But Dad and Agnes! The mention of her name was enough to put them into a full fledged battle of opinions to the exclusion of all others.

Dad, as could be expected from a farmer, did not buy any of the behavior portrayed by a red-haired, gum-chewing waif answering to the name of "Tania" and formerly Patty Hearst. He believed that you are who you are and that's that. You can't change it and neither can anyone else. He did not believe in the malarkey of any facts surrounding the case. He did not believe that you could change everything about yourself simply because you were in someone's capture.

Agnes, on the other hand, considered herself to be quite educated–we were never to forget that she was a teacher–and she felt that Dad simply did not understand brainwashing and the total effect that it could have on a person. How, if you were concerned enough about your basic survival, you would do anything and become anyone just to protect your life.

Mom and I and Hank just listened, nodding occasionally when we agreed with a particular point of view.

Agnes helped me with the dishes, never ceasing to jabber on at Dad at regular intervals. She truly felt that if he would just try to understand the process of brainwashing that he would understand how Patty Hearst had become Tania. She never did understand our dad, that was the problem. I didn't know if Patty was guilty or not guilty and I never will. But I do know that nothing on earth would ever be able to convince our father to change his identity and go against his beliefs, whether they had a gun to his head or any other part of him. And so he couldn't understand how anyone else could. Nor would I be wasting my breath trying to make him understand.

But that's what makes us all different, I decided, as I took the dredges of my tea to sit in my favorite rocking chair, looking out our big window.

Hank had driven Mama and Dad home and then headed into Brampton to pick up Mary Honey. Agnes had headed out into the cold of the December night. I was contentedly rocking and enjoying the colored lights of the Christmas tree. I guess I was like Mama. I just loved Christmas. My head lolled a little as I reveled in my solitude.

I was dreaming a little in the glow of those lights–not really asleep, but not wide awake either. I was dreaming Christmas dreams, only five days away and so much to do, but knowing there was pleasure in all of the doings, too. Mama seemed so good and that made us all happy. Hank was retrieving Mary Honey and Danny–well, Danny should be home any time now.

I smiled to myself as I thought of the joke that Danny told Hank and me just before he left. He was great at telling jokes because his face was so full of expression.

"Hey," he'd called as he was donning his coat and toque. "Did you hear about the two cannibals who were dining on a clown for dinner?"

Hank and I both shook our heads.

"One of them turned to the other and asked 'does this taste funny to you?'"

He was laughing as he shut the door, cracking himself up. Hank and I had waved at the window, grinning too.

He should be getting home any time now, I thought a little sleepily as I rocked in my comfortable chair.

I heard the sirens then. They were off in the distance but it was most unusual to hear them at all in our quiet community. At first I thought I was dreaming. I tensed and cocked my head. Then I heard them again.

My heart suddenly started thumping so hard that it hurt my ears, and my breath came in ragged gulps. I was mesmerized as I realized that those sirens were coming up our long, dark lane. Now I could see their sharp cruel lights cutting through the peace of our country night. I saw the police car trekking up towards me–and stopping at my house.

I could hear them getting out.

Someone was rapping insistently at my door.

I was alone.

I was all alone.

I was terrified.

And then slowly, slowly, slowly, like the slowest motion picture of all time, the lights on my Christmas tree went out–one by one, they extinguished into darkness. And never in my whole life did they ever shine as brightly for me again.

"There's been an accident, ma'am."

And that is the sum total of my memory of that night for quite some time. Oh, I know what happened all right. I know exactly what happened. I was to wish for the rest of my life that I could relinquish that knowledge. That for just one moment of my remaining days I could forget the events of that night. There were times, as the years wore away, that I would long for that thing of Mama's that I had dreaded so much before. That I would actually wish for the sweet numbness of mind caused by Alzheimer's. At least I wouldn't have to picture the accident over and over in my mind until I thought that I would just start screaming and never ever stop.

Danny had been going to watch a hockey game in Georgetown with our neighbours, the Wilmonts. They had a boy of the same age as Danny and he had asked if Danny could go with them on this Saturday night before Christmas. It was a local team playing, and the boys enjoyed going to cheer them on.

They'd had a good time at the game and had lingered over hot dogs and cokes, but still it wasn't late as they headed home. Not even ten o'clock. It wasn't a particularly snowy night. The roads weren't bad by December's standards.

Danny had been sitting in the front with Mr. Wilmont and John had been in the back. I have no idea why. I have wondered for almost forty years why Danny didn't sit in the back with John. Would it have made a difference? We'll never know.

The road, which is #7, connects Georgetown to our road. Before you get to our turn-off you have to go through the village of Norval, which is a very picturesque little spot and involves going down a hill and then up another hill. At the bottom of the hill is the intersection of Norval, essentially comprising four corners.

Mr. Wilmont was driving down the hill and, passing the four corners, beginning his trek upward and towards our home. A car came through the intersection without so much as slowing down and hit the front passenger side bang on. My boy was thrown through the windshield onto the cold December pavement. His neck was broken immediately.

The police were kind. The neighbours were kind. Everyone was kind and caring and concerned. And it just did not matter. I was quite sure that nothing would ever matter to me again as long as I lived.

The funeral was on Christmas Eve. I, who had always loved Christmas with all of my heart, could not bear to think of waking up on the 25th of December with no son.

When it all ended at last and we were sitting in my old living room and staring dully into the fire, I wondered if perhaps the shock and horror of all of this would actually kill my Dad. He looked as if he had aged ten years since our last meal together just last week. Mama was very quiet and seemed more bewildered than ever. Agnes was grief-stricken.

Mary Honey came into the room with a small polished wooden cross in her hands, bearing the unmistakable fastening loop of a tree ornament. She produced it tentatively. Hank turned his head away and I could see the hurt in her young eyes.

"It's to hang on the tree, Pop."

"I see that."

"It's for Danny."

Hank nodded, tears brimming in his eyes, still refusing to meet hers.

Mama held her hand out.

"Let's see, child."

Mary Honey handed it to her, with a furtive glance at me and repeated, "It's for Danny."

Mama was stroking the wood with her gentle hands.

She looked from Mary Honey to me and back to Mary Honey.

"Did you make it, dear?"

"Yes, Grandma."

Mama handed it wordlessly to me. I read "Danny Boy Dec.18 1960-Dec. 20 1975"

Mary Honey said in a flat voice, "I thought that we could hang it up beside his song on the tree. He would have liked it, I think. I mean–" and her voice trailed off now, and I had lost the ability to speak. I didn't know if Danny would have liked his own cross on the tree at all. He was fifteen years old. He would have liked to run and laugh and play hockey and start dating. He would have liked to *live*. Not lie in a cold stark coffin for eternity.

Agnes was wonderful. She was how Mama would have been if she had been all comprehending of the total situation. She could also see that the rest of us were hanging on by the very slightest of threads to our souls and our very beings.

She rose quietly and took the cross and hung it on the Christmas tree. She found the ornament with the song which Mary Honey and Mama had printed out so loving all of those years ago. The old fashioned ball which depicted his "first Christmas" she hung on the other side of the song. And that is how I have always hung them from then on. Such a brief story of such a dear, well loved boy.

"Thank you, Mary Honey," I managed to say.

"Come here," Hank said and he held out his arms for her. She just went into them.

We were such a small group it seemed now. I had never really felt that before but now we seemed pitifully few, with Mama and Dad getting so frail and only Hank and Aggie and I with Mary Honey to face the whole wide world. We sat for a long time on that Christmas Eve, too utterly exhausted and dejected and sorrowful to even move.

It was Hank who broke the silence.

"I guess we better get that light on at the end of the lane. Where's the mason jar, Hannah?"

I looked at him in total disbelief.

"I can't."

He nodded.

"I know. But we have to."

"No we don't."

"We always do."

"I don't care. It doesn't matter anymore."

"Oh yes, it does," Mama said softly. "It matters more than ever."

"It doesn't, Mama." I said sharply–sharper than I had intended. My father looked at me reproachfully and I started to cry. How could I have snapped at her?

Mama came over and put her arms around me. I was ashamed to be drawing comfort from my frail, elderly mother, but I put my head down on her shoulder nonetheless, drinking in her familiar smell and feel.

"Maybe he'll be looking for that light, Hannah," she said. "Maybe he'll be looking down hoping to see that light that he's seen every Christmas since he was just a week old."

We all just looked at her.

Sometimes she was so much like Mama–the old Mama–that it was almost unbearable. Because it was in these flashes of lucidity that we realized how much we had lost and were losing with each passing day.

We were speechless. We all just slowly got up and started getting our winter wraps on to brave the outside elements. Mary Honey found the mason jar and Agnes found the candles and with heavy, heavy hearts we headed outside to traipse across the frozen fields.

"I'm with you, sis," Agnes said, as she and I and Mary Honey were looking in the mud room for enough mittens to go around. "I'm not sure that I believe in any of this anymore."

Mary Honey paused and looked up.

"But you still believe in Christmas, Auntie Agnes, right?"

Agnes looked into her young sorrowful face and visibly softened. She sighed deeply and looked into my eyes.

I nodded wearily.

"Yes, darling girl." She replied. "I still believe in Christmas."

This was the last thing which I possess that was penned in Mama's handwriting and she handed it to me silently on that Christmas Day when Danny was so newly dead that I thought I would lay down myself and die, too.

But it has grown to be a comfort somehow. The years have done that all by themselves.

"To Parents
[This poem is a gift from Rev and Mrs. M.C. Davies
in grateful memory of their son Bryon who passed on at the
age of 17; Dec. 10, 1945]

'I'll lend to you for a little time, a child of mine,' He said.
'For you to love the while he lives and mourn for when he's dead
It may be six or seven years, or twenty two or three
But will you, till I call him back, take care of him for me?
He'll bring his charms to gladden you and shall his stay be brief
You'll have your lovely memories as solace for your grief.
I cannot promise he will stay, since all from earth return
But there are lessons taught down there, I want this child to learn
I've looked the wide world over, in search for teachers true
And from the throngs that crowd life's lane, I have selected you
Now will you give him all your love, nor think the labor vain
Nor hate Me when I call to take him back again?'
I fancied that I heard them say, "Dear Lord, Thy will be done!
For all the joy this child shall bring, the risk of grief we'll run
We'll shelter him with tenderness, we'll love him while we may
And for the happiness we've known, forever grateful stay
But should the angels call for him much sooner than we've planned
We'll brave the bitter grief that comes and try to understand."

"Where did you find this, Mama?" I turned to ask her.

But she was gone and I never found out where she found this beautiful poem.

It was enough that it was written in her own writing. I always cherished it for this and for its beautiful words.

"I still believe in Christmas today," I murmured into Hannah's beautiful fuzzy hair.

It was surprising really that I didn't hate the whole season. Every year I was reminded of his birthday and the anniversary of his death. But for some obscure reason I seemed to feel closer to him at Christmas time and the feeling increased the older I became.

I was raised in the Christian faith and I believed in the Bible. Most people of my age do. Hank and I were always very sure that we would be reunited with Danny when it was our turn to die. But I used to worry about that, too. How would I know him? He was just a boy when he died–not even fully grown. Would he stay like that? And what about us? We had aged so much. My God, I was only forty when he died. I was almost twice that now. Some mornings I didn't recognize my own self in the bathroom mirror. How was he to recognize me?

But with every year I felt better–calmer, more resigned. Perhaps it was because, in facing my own inevitable death, I was more accepting of things. And as year after year passed I knew, without a shadow of a doubt, that no matter how old I was I would always know my boy. He was my own-from my own body and blood and I knew that I would know him anywhere. That was the wonderful gift that old age had given me.

I always hung Danny's ornaments close to my chair so that I could easily see them and once a year I would sing that beautiful old ballad. I sang it for my boy. And I sang it for me.

My voice was getting old and cracked. My hair was grey and my face was lined. But when I sang that song, all alone in my rocking chair, I was a young mother again with a bouncing baby boy clinging to me.

"And if you come, when all the flowers are dying
And I am dead, as dead I well may be
You'll come and find the place where I am lying
And kneel and say an "Ave" there for me
And I shall hear, tho' soft you tread above me
And all my dreams will warm and sweeter be
If you'll not fail to tell me that you love me
I'll simply sleep in peace until you come to me."

That was the last verse that Mary Honey and Mama had penned on the back of the ornament so many, many years ago. And they were so appropriate now. I found a strange comfort in singing the song every year. I felt as if I were singing it just for my boy.

It was not a hardship to get older when I realized that I would be with him again. And my Mama. She was the reason that I hadn't succumbed to my sorrow that year. In a very odd roundabout way she had given me the strength to keep on going.

It had been early spring, just a few short months after Danny had died that I had been making my way across the familiar fields to the old farmhouse where Mama and dad had lived as long as I could ever recall. My heart was so heavy that I could hardly walk around with it in my chest. I felt dark with sadness. It was pure chance really that I had tripped on an old piece of stubble left over in the field. I tripped and fell onto my back. It was late afternoon and a dreary day. I simply didn't get back on my feet again. I just stayed there, lying on my back and gazing dully into the grey sky. I wasn't hurt. I just wasn't inspired to move a muscle.

I have no idea how long I lay there. Mary Honey was away for the whole day and Hank had gone to an auction sale in Caledon East. I had told my mother the day before that I would be over for an afternoon cup of tea but often she didn't even remember these arrangements. I felt a strange, eerie sense of total peace taking over my body as I just lay there and lay there, looking at the oppressing sky that was darkening around me.

How pleasant, how very pleasant. I remember thinking this, as I lay there. I felt that I could just be still until I melted into the field and the earth and became nothing at all. I wouldn't feel any pain or sorrow or loss ever again. I would be free from my earthly ties.

They were just keeping me here, anyway, and away from my only son.

It wasn't so much an act of aggression as of passivity. I didn't want to *do* anything to myself. I didn't want to take any action against my life. I just wanted to lie very still until the life drained from me and the cold seeped in and I didn't have any feeling left inside of me. I would just be numb. I was already numb inside.

Darkness was descending more quickly now. I could actually see a star or two above me. I closed my eyes in supreme peace.

And then I heard my name being called through the cool country evening.

"Hannah! Hannah!"

I kept my eyes closed and pretended to myself that I hadn't heard.

"Hannah!"

Oh, God. It was Mama. I opened my eyes reluctantly, leaving behind my new found peace and facing the sadness again with a heavy, heavy heart. Slowly I sat up and saw my mother rushing over to me through the fields. She didn't even have a sweater on over her light cotton top. I felt a stab of guilt like a dagger drive through me.

"I'm here, Mama," I said weakly, waving my hands at her.

Her expression was one of utter joy as she saw me. She quickened her pace and crossed the field swiftly until she knelt at my side. My mothers' mind may have been questionable at times, but her body was as spry as ever.

She grabbed my hands and sat down on the cold earth beside me.

"Mama, what on earth are you doing out here without a jacket?" I reprimanded her. "You'll catch your death of a cold. And Dad'll have a fit."

"He's doing chores. And I'm fine. What are *you* doing out here lying on the ground? Are you okay?"

"Yes, Mama. I'm fine. I just tripped on some old stubble, is all."

"Well, why didn't you get up, child? Did you hurt your ankle?"

I shook my head and I was angry beyond words to find tears filling my eyes and spilling onto my cheeks. Sometimes Mama seemed so much like herself that it was hard to imagine that she was another person altogether. That was the true crime of Alzheimer's–not to take a person totally, but to leave just enough that it broke your heart anew with each new day.

Mama didn't say anything. She just took me in her arms and rocked me. I felt absolutely miserable to be taking comfort from her yet again. I should be the strong one. I said as much but Mama just tsk'ed me and rocked me and told me that everything was going to be all right. I might have to wait but she promised that it would be. She promised with her whole heart and soul.

I was completely and utterly ashamed of myself.

I lifted my head and looked into her kind, blue eyes. I could see the love for me shining from them like a beacon that would never fade.

"I'm so sorry, Mama. " I whispered.

"I know. I know." She murmured.

Then she sat up straight and, taking my face in her loving hands, she looked straight into my soul and said, "Hannah?"

"Yes, Mama."

"We've lost Danny."

"I know, Mama."

She sighed deeply and went on.

"We've lost Danny," she repeated slowly as if trying to understand this herself.

"And I'm losing my mind." She sighed again and relaxed her hold on my face, dropping her hands into her lap and looking down, as if embarrassed by the admission.

She looked at me searchingly and I nodded my assent with deep sorrow. In an astonishing moment of clarity, she reached her hands up and held my face again. She looked at me almost fiercely. She did not pretend a lack of understanding as to why I had been lying outside in a cold farmer's field for the better part of the afternoon. She just said in a strangled voice that sounded as if it were being wrenched from her throat.

"I can't lose you, too, Hannah. I just can't."

And so my mother didn't lose me. She never did.

But I lost her. Bit by agonizing bit I lost her until she was nothing but a shell–a shadow of her former self. Some days she didn't even know me or Agnes.

She'd been so lucid that day out in the cold dark field. As I look back that was the last time that I remember her being like the old Mama. She saved me from myself but I could not save her.

Agnes eventually moved to Kingston to expand her teaching career. It was only a few hours away but I missed her acutely. She tried to come back every month or so but Mama really grew away from her in those years. It upset Agnes greatly not to be a part of our day-to-day lives. For a person who is struggling with their own mind and memory, a lot of their fragile hold on things is based on day-to day-routine. Just by virtue of distance Agnes was no longer a part of that daily round of life. However, a person has to live her own life, and our mother would have been the very first person in the world to have acknowledged this–when she was our mother.

The day which I will always remember as the beginning of the end was the day that I walked across the fields with supper for her and Dad. I tried to do this as much as I could. My dad still farmed part of the farm and had a hundred head of cattle, so he was out doing chores when I made my familiar way into our old kitchen.

Mama was sitting at the table with a cup of tea and a slice of banana bread that I had delivered the previous day. Dad had wrapped her up in a blanket and she certainly looked comfy enough. If it weren't for the blankness in her face, one would have thought that she was doing all right. But her expression betrayed her-or rather, her total lack of expression.

She turned that face to me now and I felt a sharp stab at my heart as I realized that she was unsure of my identity. I smiled at her reassuredly but her eyes still held a certain degree of fear.

"He's-he's out in the barn," she stammered.

"Who?" I asked.

She shrugged as the name would not come to her.

I sat down at the table and took her face in my hands, as she had so often done to me. She looked so old and sad. I gazed into her faded blue eyes.

"Don't you know who I am?" I asked gently.

She looked at me and tried to think. Then with a deep sigh she looked away and shook her head.

"I don't know." She said simply and sighed again.

"I remember that I love you," she whispered this uncertainly and did not meet my eyes.

I dropped her face and tried to smile at her.

"I love you too, Mama," I said brokenly.

I began to busy myself with supper preparations.

That was the day that I talked to my father about nursing home provisions. He was aging daily with the burden of looking after a frail wife. I had not realized that there was a great portion of each day in which she had no recognition of him. He had kept this strictly to himself for as long as possible. My dad was a proud man and believed in keeping his troubles a private matter. But I was beginning to worry about Mama's safety as more and more she wandered at night. Several times she had left the stove on and almost caused a fire. My dad was exhausted and care worn.

At first, of course, he would have no part in any dealings with any nursing home. I had expected this reaction and was gentle as I broached the unwelcome topic. However, as the months wore on and my mother's general health deteriorated he began to resign himself to the inevitable. I could see that it broke his heart, though.

I began the proceedings with Dr. Morrison. I could tell that it saddened him as well, but he tried to be positive and he was definitely approving of the decision. [He, in fact, told me that he had tried to convince my father for several years that my mother should be placed, but my dad would not even consider the possibility.] There were several nursing homes in our area. Brampton and Mississauga were both quite close and we would be able to visit her every day. The only thing that made my father consider the possibility of a nursing home were my promises that I would do just that, even several times daily if need be. In my heart I really did not want Mama to leave the farmhouse where she had lived for so long and been so happy. I knew that it was breaking Dad's heart a little every day and I started to worry about his health as well. But I was more worried that she would get out one night as Dad slept and freeze to death or run out on the road. The irony did not escape me that if this happened that I could quite easily come across her in much the same situation that she had found me that miserable spring after Danny died.

We wanted her safe. That was the bottom line as those annoying visiting nurses and nursing home personnel were so fond of saying. We did want her safe–of course we did–but it was killing us all the same to think of placing her somewhere away from her beloved farm.

Summer was approaching quickly and summer is a busy, busy time on a farm. We–Dad and Agnes and I–made our final decision in July when a bed became vacant at the Extendicare Nursing Home in Mississauga. It was a two hundred-bed nursing home located right across the street from Mississauga's General Hospital. Many of the residents were hospital outpatients who were recuperating and I suspect that Dr. Morrison may have pulled some strings in securing the bed. Anyway, a bed came up and would be available on the first of August if we so desired.

It is one thing to talk about placement in the abstract. It is quite another thing when that prospect becomes a reality.

So with heavy, heavy hearts we accepted the bed at Extendicare and started making arrangements to move our mom there.

It was summer and so Agnes was off. The only thing that kept me going was the presence and support of my sister and I suspect the same was true for her–although, being Agnes, she would never admit to that.

We started the first week of July sorting things out at the old farmhouse. There was a lifetime of stuff. It was very difficult to know what to do, but we persevered.

On the 15th of July 1980 Agnes and I took a coffee break from our labors to sit with Mama who was sitting blankly in front of the television set. The Olympics were supposed to open on Saturday in Moscow but several countries were boycotting them. The United States, West Germany and Japan were protesting the military intervention of the Soviet Union in Afghanistan. I was entering the room with a tray of cookies and soda bread when I heard Agnes gasp.

"Hannah! Never mind the tray. Come and look at this."

I was not too worried. Agnes got much more excited about current events than I did. I thought that there must be a new development in Moscow. I carefully put the tray down and sat beside Mama on the old chintz chesterfield.

And I watched the top story unfolding on our local news channel of a huge fire in the Extendicare Nursing Home in Mississauga. It had started the previous evening and had quickly escalated into a deadly disaster.

They did not know the exact cause of the fire but it was suspected that one of the seniors on the top floor had been smoking. Although smoking was forbidden it was still known to happen at times.

It didn't matter how it started–not to any of us, sitting there holding Mama close to us. The damage was extensive. People in the neighborhood tried to help and firefighters did save some lives using ropes and ladders. But in the end thirty-five people were injured and twenty-one people lost their lives.

Agnes and I were speechless. And horrified. And resigned.

Dad took it as a sign that Mama was not to be placed at all and that was that.

And in the end it didn't matter. It just ended, on its own–in Mama's home where she had been so happy and loving to all of us, wanting only our happiness and love in return.

It was September of that year when I slipped over one golden afternoon to be with her. Dad had taken a much needed break to attend a cattle show with some other old farmers. Agnes had gone back to school and life had slowed to a comfortable pace.

I walked quietly into my old home, not wanting to startle Mama. Dad had wrapped her up in her favorite old blanket and I approached her softly to drop a kiss on her beloved cheek.

I noted immediately her unnatural stillness and my heart skipped a beat. Her cheek was ice cold.

She was gone. Her spirit had slipped away into a place where there was no memory loss and only love and beauty such as she had always bestowed on those of us who were lucky enough to have her. Mama was at peace. I hoped with all of my heart that she was with Danny. She had loved him so very much.

Even though we had been losing bits and pieces of her along the years, Agnes and I were still devastated by her death. She was only seventy-five years old. It seemed far too young. I knew there were people who lost their mothers much earlier in life. Still, though, I didn't think that a person who was so inherently good and kind should have to leave us like this. As Mary Honey used to say when she was a little girl "It's not *fair!*"

My poor dad just never really survived without her–literally. It was only a matter of a few weeks later that he was rushed to hospital and succumbed to a major heart attack. This, surprisingly, brought me little sorrow for I knew that he was most unhappy living in the world without Mama. She was his whole reason for living and nothing could bring him any comfort after she left.

Years and years later [quite recently actually] someone spoke to me about a "broken-hearted syndrome" which actually exists in people who have had a major loss. It is called "takotsubo" syndrome. Apparently there is a sudden temporary weakness of the myocardium [heart wall] triggered by emotional stress and it can cause acute heart failure. Of course, no one knew these things in the early '80s, but Hank and I knew for certain that my dad did indeed die of a broken heart. When I heard this information related to me and I had a chance to mull it over in my mind I wondered why I hadn't myself died–especially if this was affecting mainly women, as I had discovered. I hadn't, though... Danny was gone. Mama and Dad were gone. Part of me was gone, too, but the rest of me just struggled on and on. Mary Honey needed me so much. I had to keep on.

It was sad, though, to lose both of my parents in such a short space of time. When Mama died she took so much from us–even though she wasn't really herself the last few years, she still made up the whole world for me and Agnes and Mary Honey, and of course, my dad.

Hank and I moved into the beloved farmhouse and settled into it with all of the loving memories that were steeped into its walls. I loved living there and I still love it today. Our house had great memories as well, but I was still able to sell it. I never, ever could have sold the farmhouse. It was a part of my very being.

I looked at the sleeping baby of present day nestled in my arms and said, "That was the end of my Mama's story, Baby Hannah. I wish that you could have known her. She was your great-great-grandma and she was amazing. But something really wonderful happened in 1979. It turned out to be the beginning of your very own story."

1979

The International Year of the Child

By 1979, of course, Hallmark was well on its way to making Christmas ornaments for the tree and they've never looked back. Today you can get an ornament for pets, graduation, new baby, wedding, engagements and just about anything at all.

The 1979 "Baby's First Christmas" is a threaded ball, built to withstand the years–and it has.

As I look back I think that the only thing that kept me living and breathing every day was that little girl that merited the 1979 ball. Her name was Olivia Mary Hannah and she was my first, my last and my only grandchild.

She came at a time when my world was very sad. Mama didn't know me, Dad was bent forever under a care worn world from which he never actually escaped, Danny was gone and Mary Honey was with someone Hank and I did not like very much. That sounds awful when I say it out loud now, but it was true.

After Danny died I know that I lost a lot of myself and I know that Mary Honey also was robbed-first of a beloved brother and then of her grandparents. Hank and I were still there but we were not and never would be the same family circle for her. Some days it was all I could do to drag my heartsick bones out of bed. Mary Honey was twenty-one years old when Danny died. She was an adult and already well on her way to a teaching career. I seem to have been walking around with blinders on just trying to survive every day. When I awoke to reality-gradually, oh so gradually, Mary Honey was engaged to a man we hadn't even met.

That woke me up for sure, as did the fact that he didn't really *want* to meet us. Hank thought this very suspect indeed. Mary Honey told us by herself that she was pregnant and that she would be getting married very quietly at the town hall in Brampton. Of course they wanted us there, she had added hastily.

She had been living on her own in Brampton and had never really brought a serious boyfriend home to meet us. Neither Hank nor I knew that this man even existed.

"Well, where is he?" Hank asked, his tone harsh. "Why isn't he here with you now? Shouldn't he be at least meeting us, for Christ sake?"

I looked warningly at him. I did not want hard feelings now. Mary Honey looked so small and vulnerable–not at all like someone who was giving us happy news. She looked beaten.

"Peter's a little shy, Dad," she said falteringly.

"Shy? Shy?' His voice was a roar now.

"Yes. He's a shy guy and he is worried about meeting you."

"And why would that be, I wonder? Huh? Maybe because he's a God damned–"

"Hank!" Now my voice was sharp as I cut off what I could only imagine was coming next.

Hank got up and left the room without another word.

I was in shock. This was not how we were. It was so rare that there were any hard words at all in our home that I felt sick. Nothing on earth had prepared me for this situation.

I got up and sat down beside Mary Honey. I took her hand tentatively and said "I'm going to be a grandma?"

"Yes, Mom."

"Are you happy about all this?"

She nodded her head but the tears that crept into her eyes and slipped silently down her cheeks belied her words. I put my arms around her and held her.

"I miss him, Mom. I miss him so much."

"I know. I know. We'll always miss him."

I was her mom-I did not have to ask who "him" was. It was the "him" that I missed, too. Every day with every beat of my heart.

Not a word about Peter or an engagement or a baby. That was how Hank found us when he came in later on. All of the anger had left him. He sat down on the other side of our dear girl and also put his arms around her. We were such a small family now. I wondered if I would ever get used to that.

"You don't have to marry this guy just because you're going to have a baby," Hank said. "Your mother and I will help you. You must know that."

"I know. But I do love Peter. You'll like him. Just wait and see."

"Mary Honey," and Hanks' voice was very gentle now. "Why isn't he here with you right now?"

"I told you, Dad. He's shy."

"Nobody's *that* shy."

"He is." And a stubborn edge had crept into her tone.

And Hank, blessedly, said nothing more.

Sometimes when the wheels of life are in motion there is just no turning back. You have to play out the days that dot your own personal calendar of life even when you can see that heartache lies ahead just as surely as those months lie ahead on the calendar. But still what choice do we have in the end? We can't just lie down in the cold, wet fields and surrender. That would be too, too easy.

Because it doesn't take someone with psychic abilities to figure out that a man who would not be forthcoming to meet a girl's parents when she was pregnant and young and vulnerable was not going to be a mainstay in her life.

However, we went through all of those motions–the wedding and the new home and the settling in of a young marriage. I have always thought that if you have to try too hard to like someone that perhaps the effort could be better used elsewhere.

But I did not want to waste an extra moment of any day dwelling on Peter. As the kids say now, he was a "loser."

I looked at the little one and kissed her fuzzy head for the millionth time.

"Out of all of these dark days came something really wonderful, Hannah darling. Your mother came to us. She just lit up our lives when she was born and she has ever since. And now we have you. You are the future, my little love."

The year of the child. It seemed like a perfect year to welcome a new baby into our family, somehow. It seemed good and right, even if we were less than pleased about that baby's father.

"Every Child" was a short animated film, commemorating the year of the child which entailed a child who was rejected from every house until she was taken in by two tramps who gave her love and tenderness. There is a whole lesson in there which I never explored too much. I was just too busy getting my own little world ready for my own little one.

I had forgotten totally how all consuming the love of a new baby could be. In the midst of my life it was sadness that had become the marking of our daily life-with Danny's loss and Mama's illness and Agnes moving away.

A baby shone like a beacon that was brilliant and loving. My life was illuminated now and never again did I lose myself to darkness and despair. Some people have so many grandchildren that they have to stop and count them up. Some brag about the quantities they have acquired as if they were personal achievements. We only ever had Olivia and she meant the whole world to Hank and me. She always did and she always will.

"Your mommy, Hannah," I rocked and smiled at the memory of the perfect happiness which Olivia brought with her and which has stayed with us until this present day.

We always made our Christmas Eve trek out the lane to leave our candle glowing in the darkness for our little world. The years following Danny's death, though, we had done it with heavy hearts and weary feet-more out of a blind faith than anything else.

But Christmas 1979–that Christmas Eve the walk was again instilled with all of the holiday joy we had lost bit by bit along the years. Olivia was nine months old and she was old enough to be excited and cheerful about the night sky and the colored lights. She clapped her hands with glee as we stuck the mason jar in the white frozen snow bank and lit the candle. Hank linked his arm through mine and we all laughed with the happiness that only a baby can bring–that happiness that is all new as if seeing things for the very first time.

We were glad to light the Christmas way for our new girl. We were glad to be her grandparents and we looked forward to spending as much of her little life with her as we could.

It turns out that this resulted in quite a bit of time. Mary Honey found herself alone with her child very early on in her marriage. She had secured a teaching job in Georgetown. Hank and I, therefore, were in a perfect location to have Olivia dropped on our doorstep every day that Mary Honey taught school.

Those years just slipped away. I was to learn that time only dragged when life was misery and loss. When life was full of joy the time went quickly-as if it were quicksilver–as if you would like to hold out your hands and slow it down. Having a granddaughter was pure and utter joy, which of course made our lives the same. I read a quote one day in a coffee table book and it read, "How we spend our days is, of course, how we spend our lives."

How we spent our lives was with Olivia Mary Hannah-quite a large handle for such a little girl.

I chuckled as I surveyed my Christmas tree of present day and reflected how it would be considerably barer if we'd not had that little maid. I had saved some of Mary Honey's ornaments as well, of course. At least a half a dozen of hers adorned my tree. But with Olivia I couldn't bear to part with any of them. Any little thing that she had made in any form of decoration at all found its inexorable way to some branch of my tree. Perhaps I had grown mellower–perhaps I just didn't mind anymore–more likely I was more attuned to how fragile life actually was, and how we have to cherish every scrap made us by our loving girl who was growing up like a little whirlwind all around us.

Mary Honey and Hank and I kept her well versed in Christmas knowledge as well. We didn't want Mama's legacy to go by the wayside after all her years of Christmas research. When Agnes came up from Kingston for her Christmas visit we would be more than prepared for her. It got to be again the fun-filled game that it had been with Mama and I was glad that it hadn't died with her. It was always good to have knowledge. And Christmas knowledge was our specialty. We had decided that many years ago, Mama and I. We were Christmas people.

"Why do we write Xmas?"

"The X in Xmas stands for the Greek letter *chi*, the first letter in the Greek word for Christ. Gradually the letter X came to stand for the name of Christ. It's not taking Christ out of Christmas, as some think."

"What does the actual word Christmas come from then?"

"An old English phrase that means "Mass of Christ."

"What is the shape of candy canes designed to represent?"

"The crooks of shepherds."

"What are the three wise men called?"

"The magi."

"But what are their names?"

"No idea."

"Balthasar. Melchior. Gaspar."

"Olivia darling, this one's for you. What did Frosty the Snowman put on that made him come alive?"

"An old straw hat, Aunt Agnes. I'm not a baby."

"And this one, dear sister, is for you. What is the name of the angel in *It's a Wonderful Life*?"

"And I, like Olivia, am not a baby. Clarence Oddbody, I believe, is that angel. As two to be exact."

"Okay, now you've lost me," Agnes had to admit.

"Angel second class."

"Oh I see! Second class, you say."

"Yes, Aggie dear, because he doesn't have his wings yet."

Agnes shook her head. She did not like to be outdone, especially by myself, a little country mouse who rarely left the farm.

"You love that old movie, don't you, Granny?"

"I do, my love. If I didn't watch it at Christmas, well it just wouldn't be Christmas that's all."

"Every year. It's painful," Hank complained.

"Indeed." I turned to my sister and daughter and granddaughter [poor Hank was quite outnumbered]. "One year we missed it and he kept asking why we hadn't watched it."

"That sounds like you, Pop," Mary Honey laughed.

"You can get used to anything, even hanging, as my old uncle used to say." Hank grinned.

"So," he continued, amused. "What happens when a bell rings?"

"An angel gets his wings." We all answered in unison, even Olivia. She silently pointed to a little Christmas sign on my kitchen window sill. It proclaimed that very sentiment.

"Your granny has so many Christmas decorations and signs and lights I can't keep track of them all."

"That sign always makes me think of Mama," I said softly.

"It does?" Agnes didn't see it. Sometimes when people can't see things on their own there is not too much point in explaining them, but I made an attempt.

"She's like our Christmas angel. She always loved the whole season so much. I feel so close to her at Christmas."

"And Uncle Danny. He's a Christmas angel too, isn't he, Granny?"

Mary Honey looked at her warningly, but I didn't want to be someone whom others had to watch their words around.

"He sure is, love. He died just a few days before Christmas."

"Is that why we leave a candle in the snow for him?"

"Partly," Hank replied. "But we've been leaving a light on for Christmas since before even your mom was born, Olivia."

"That's a long time." She sighed and we all laughed.

"It's a tradition now," Agnes agreed. "It's just a part of Christmas, that's all. We wouldn't be able to go to bed if we didn't stick that silly old mason jar out in the snow bank."

"I think that our loved ones would be lost, just searching for that Christmas light," I sighed and laughed a little to show that I was half-joking.

"I remember that Mama thought so, anyways." Agnes said. "When Danny died and we were all so despondent she made us traipse down the old lane with our candle and leave it in the snow."

I thought of that sad Christmas when we made the journey to the end of the lane with our mason jar and our heavy, heavy hearts. And somehow, it had felt better to light that candle in the frosty snow bank and leave it there in our corner of the world. Was it just because Mama believed that Danny was seeking comfort from that little light in the big dark night? I don't know. But somehow, somewhere I hoped that it was shining brightly for both of them.

1983

The year of the Cabbage Patch

I had the whole long winter evening to sit in my chair, rocking my new baby. I chuckled to myself as my eyes rested on the cloth quilted ornament from 1983. It was a likeness of a Cabbage Patch doll which had been purchased already, appliqued on fabric and stitched together by myself to form an ornament. They certainly had been a hot item that year.

Hank and I had been out for an afternoon drive in the spring of that year. We didn't often really have time to shop together, and it was only a fluke that found us standing in the Towers store in Orangeville looking at a silly fabric doll with a pinched up face and hair fashioned from yellow yarn and tied with pink bows. I had wandered into the toy department and was actually looking at puzzles for Olivia. She loved to puzzle and I thought that it was good for her mind. Hank, however, seemed fascinated by this shelf of dolls.

"Hannah, look at this. Aren't these dolls cute?"

"I guess so. I guess they're so ugly they're cute. Cabbage patch kids," I read the notice out loud. "I never heard of them."

"They're kind of unique." The woman who was stacking toys down the aisle turned to address us. “They were first created by Xavier Roberts and he produced them through Babyland General Hospital down in Cleveland Georgia two years ago. The idea was that he displayed them in a hospital setting and that you could adopt them. No two are alike and each one comes with adoption papers. They are already named and have a birthday and you have to register them.”

“Oh, wow. I can’t say I’m familiar with them at all,” I admitted.

“You may be hearing more about them this year. Coleco bought the rights to them last year and so they are being mass produced. Some retailers say that they will be a huge hit this Christmas.”

We listened politely but we never had been too interested in fads or things like that. And it was only early April. Christmas seemed a long time away.

Hank, though, was inexorably impressed with one particular doll posing there among the other yellow and green boxes. I peered at her more closely and read the “adoption papers” displayed in the plastic window encasing her.

“Olivia Mary,” I read. I could see that Hank was duly impressed.

“Oh, for heaven’s sake, Hank. It’s just a coincidence.”

“Coincidence,” he said thoughtfully. “I don’t know. She has strawberry blonde hair and blue eyes. And, Hannah, look at her birthday: March 8th.”

“And she’s $25.88, Hank. I don’t even think Olivia’s much into dolls. She’s already had her birthday this year.”

“Yes, I guess you’re right at that,” Hank agreed.

These were still times when people were concerned about “spoiling” children with too many material things.

I honestly never gave that funny looking doll a second thought. It was a couple of weeks later that Hank came home with a big plastic bag under his arm and a sheepish grin on his face. Olivia was helping me make an apple crisp in the kitchen and he skulked quietly up the creaky old stairs and into our room to deposit the parcel before he reappeared for his floury kiss from both of us.

It was later on when we were sitting down with our evening cup of tea that he admitted to the purchase of the "Olivia Mary" Cabbage Patch Kid.

"I'd forgotten about that silly thing entirely," I told him.

I couldn't imagine that he himself had given it a second thought. Hank usually left the entire gift buying and such up to me completely.

"We can save it for Christmas," he said a little defiantly. "I just really like the idea of her having the same name and birthday. It seems like it should be Livy's–that's all."

"You are incorrigible." I laughed and never gave her a second thought. She was way at the back of my clothes closet and that's where she stayed for months.

Now, anyone who remembers the Christmas of 1983 will have to remember the uproar of the Cabbage Patch Kids. In the fall I heard rumblings about them, and by December there were out and out wars in department stores regarding these goofy looking dolls with their individual names and birthdays and funny looking faces. They were on the news and advertisements everywhere. People were actually lining up and fighting and pulling them out of other shoppers' arms. There were all kinds of stories about battles over the "kids."

Of course, it is human nature to want what is out of reach and unattainable. That is how the world goes around. And so it was quite predictable that four-year-old Olivia would desire a Cabbage Patch Kid for Christmas. And when you are four you have complete and utter faith in the Santa, who is magic and has access to anything anywhere.

Mary Honey was despairing of this one afternoon to Hank and me as Olivia was getting her toys picked up to go home.

"You would think that she'd be too young to even know which toy is all the rage. But they pick it up from commercials and things. And her little pal at the babysitters wants one for Christmas too. You just can't get them anywhere. I've phoned all over and asked around. But everyone is looking for one. It's kind of silly, really, when you think about it. Last year it was those stupid ET dolls and now they're everywhere. I don't care really, but I'd like to get one for Livy if I could. It's the only thing that she says she wants for Christmas."

"I might know where there's one." Hank said thoughtfully, as if racking his brain.

"Don't tease me, Pops." Mary Honey's tone was uncharacteristically sharp.

She looked tired, my poor girl. It is a rough road being a single mom. Hank and I helped all that we could and Olivia went to the babysitters only rarely. But nothing really makes up for the lack of a loving partner. Hank and I did what we could to fill the gap for her, but we both knew that she was often sad and lonesome.

I went over and rubbed her shoulders tenderly. She turned and planted a kiss on my rough old hand. I smiled at her mischievously.

"Actually, your dad isn't teasing this time. He really does have one of those kids, you know."

"How on earth could Pops get one when no one else in Brampton or Georgetown or even Toronto seems to be able to locate one?"

Hank grinned at her.

"You need to have more faith in your old dad. I just picked it up in my travels. I don't spend all of my time here and at work, you know."

I could see Mary Honey starting to look interested.

"You do realize, don't you, that people are lining up at department stores and fighting over those silly dolls?"

"Well, that's just not very Christmassy now, is it?" Hanks' tone was maddenly calm and I could see that Mary Honey was not one hundred per cent convinced of the authenticity of his claim.

"Dad, please don't tease me," she begged.

"I'm not, dear heart. I'm not. I promise on my honour that I have a genuine Cabbage Patch Kid that will be Olivia's on Christmas morning and it even has her name and birthday on it."

Now Mary Honey just shook her head and looked at me.

"Is it true, Mom? Don't lie to me."

"My God, child, when have we ever lied to you, I'd like to know?"

"I know that you wouldn't, Mom but Dad has been known to, well, to tease, you know."

Hank tried his best to look stricken but he was actually too darned pleased with himself to wipe the grin off his face. He was the man of the hour and he knew it. I hadn't thought anything at all of those silly old dolls with their funny looking faces and in reality neither had he until he saw the name and birth date on her tag.

But credit where credit was due. He was the one who bought the doll way back in the spring and he was one happy grandpa on Christmas morning when Olivia Mary opened her bright package and found a most coveted Cabbage Patch Kid.

That was also the year that Agnes had exciting memories to add to our repertoire of little stories. She had been in Ottawa during the summer of that year when Prince Charles and Lady Diana had visited and she was smitten. This was no small thing for my self-assured sister. She was much worldlier than I and considered herself to be quite a professional woman having done very well in her teaching career. There was never any doubt in my or Mary Honey's mind that Agnes was an excellent teacher. After all, she could make you think that she was absolutely, for certain sure correct in her way of thinking even if you started out thinking that she was absolutely, for certain sure wrong.

But oh, my, my, she was thrilled beyond anything when she saw Lady Di. Agnes taught in Kingston and so was quite able to drive to our fair capital city and was lucky enough to shake that fair princess's hand. She loved that Diana had been a teacher and that she loved children and that she apparently could sign to some of the disabled little ones.

Olivia listened with awe as she told her about seeing and touching a real princess. Olivia was only four, though, and her Cabbage Patch was her first love. Hence the little quilted ornament depicting the year of the Cabbage Patch. It's very sad to tell, but Lady Di's ornament didn't grace our tree until 1997 when she died so tragically in Paris. That one I still hang every year, too. It was purchased from Hallmark. [Really, I have done my part in keeping them in business haven't I?] And I like it to remind me of our fair, kind princess. I always think that she would be so proud of her boys if she could know them now. But perhaps she does know. Perhaps. I hope so.

I smile now as I reflect that 1983 does not sound like such a long time ago.

Mama would have liked the essence of Princess Diana and loved that Agnes was able to meet her. Mama loved anyone who was good and kind, probably because she was the epitome of goodness and kindness itself. She would have been less thrilled with the hype and publicity that accompanied those silly old Kids with their lovably ugly faces. But she would have liked, very much, the pleasure which our Olivia gleaned from that doll which bore her name.

Olivia still has that doll to this day, and that gives me pleasure as well. Someday Baby Hannah will play with that doll, I'm quite sure. It's funny to think that Hank felt the urge to retrieve her from the Towers shelf way back in the spring before anyone really knew much about Cabbage Patch Kids.

I chuckle to myself when I think of how smug Hank became over that particular purchase.

Olivia Mary. March 8th. It does make you wonder, now, doesn't it?

There is a little freckled girl with red pigtails, a green old fashioned frock, luminous grey eyes and a huge smile who peeks out of the branches of my tree every year and wants you to love her, even though she's not a boy. I always place her just a little inwards so that she is comfy and has a good spot to look out between the fragrant needles. She is as Canadian as the new maple leaf flag, and she took up residence in my heart when I was twelve years old. She is as real to me as some folk whom I've known in my real life.

She is, of course, Anne of Green Gables. I always felt particularly close to her because her creator, the legendary L.M. Montgomery, lived for some time in our little village of Norval and by all accounts was very happy there. Norval lay in very close proximity to our farm and it was where we often walked and shopped. Mama sang in the choir of the Norval United Church.

L.M.Montgomery, who was also known as Mrs. Ewan McDonald, the Presbyterian Ministers' wife, was my hero. I couldn't believe that she had actually lived so close to my own home and that Mama and Dad had even spoken to her. She left Norval the year that I was born–1935–and she died in 1942 but that hadn't stopped me from badgering Mama when I was a youngster about those bygone days.

"But what was she like, Mama? What was she really like?" I would plead with Mama, usually fresh from a read of Anne and longing to know more about the woman who had made her so alive for me.

Mama was always busy doing something but she was never too busy to talk to her girls, even if this was not the first time she'd been asked this particular question.

"Well, Hannah, you know she was just an ordinary person. She was a minister's wife and so she was always busy in the community and always out socially. She was great at recitals and getting up plays. I think that she was very well thought of; she was a good- living woman."

This was probably an outdated expression even at the time when Mama was using it, but I knew what it meant. It meant that she was a good example and stayed close to hearth and home and tried to uphold the church teachings.

"I'm sure that she was just lovely. I wish that I'd known her."

"She was an ordinary woman, Hannah," Mama repeated.

"How could she be ordinary if she wrote the Anne books?"

"Well, she was a very talented writer, for sure," Mama conceded. "Mark Twain said that Anne was the sweetest creation of child life ever written."

"Mama. How do you know these things?"

"Hannah, it's quoted on the cover of the book and you've usually got it out somewhere or other," Mama said this a little dryly but with a tiny grin.

I was not to be squelched and replied a little loftily that Mark Twain had been absolutely right.

I loved Anne. I loved the way she was and the way she looked at things and I would picture for hours what it would be like to live in Prince Edward Island near the ocean. Agnes had read the novel but she did not love it as I did. It wasn't that she disliked it. She just didn't "make a religion out of it," as she informed me. It was different for me. I loved Anne with my whole heart. Mama said it was because Agnes had too little imagination and I had too much. Mama always did have a lot of insight.

I related to the red-headed heroine even in our names. I felt that the "h" on the end of my name was somewhat akin to the "e" which Anne was famous for. I began to declare that my name was "Hannah with an h."

The first time I said this in my father's hearing he had looked bewilderingly at Mama and asked, "Is there another way to spell it?"

Mama said gently, "She means at the end, dear."

Mama knew. She had read the book and understood the importance of how the written name is presented. My father was a down-to-earth farmer and would not have understood the novel if someone had purchased Coles Notes and personally read them aloud to him. He was still mystified.

"The end?"

"The 'h' on the end of Hannah's name, dear. She thinks it looks nicer than spelling it without it."

"Can you actually spell it without an 'h' on the end?" He looked around at us questioningly. Agnes shrugged. She was like him. She could not see any importance of such a discussion. I had rolled my eyes heavenward.

Dad was serious, though. He turned to my mom.

"I mean really, Beth–can you? It's not like the name Anne. You can spell that with or without an 'e' but I've never seen Hannah spelt without an 'h'."

Mama and Aggie and I all dissolved into laughter at this point, much to my fathers' chagrin. He was so totally innocent, my father. He declared that he was going to the barn to milk the cows who were easier to understand than "us women."

It was, of course, Mama who fashioned the little replica of Anne for me to trim the tree with. There is no date on her as she is really a little cloth doll and so she represents to me a lot of my girlhood years when I felt so close to the little red-head. She is like a dear friend, a kindred spirit, to quote Anne herself.

I thought for sure that Mary Honey would love her as I did, but she never warmed to the Montgomery books that adorned my books shelves. She liked to read but she liked the Hardy Boys and Nancy Drew and felt my little Canadian heroine to be quite "wishy-washy" actually. It had never occurred to me that my daughter would not love her as I did, but I continued to keep her close to my own heart. It would not be unusual for me to pick up the old, worn copy of "Anne" and read scraps of it to myself, no matter what age I was.

In 1985 Kevin Sullivan produced and directed a movie based on the famous book and I knew most certainly that I would not like it. I could not imagine condensing a book of such magnitude and words into a movie, even if it was extended length. I was not interested in watching it, and I could not imagine that Lucy Maud would have approved of such an undertaking.

It was on Christmas morning 1986 that I found a VHS copy of this very movie wrapped and underneath my tree from Olivia. She was almost eight years old and had expressed an interest in the pert little miss with red hair who sat loftily on my Christmas pine. Olivia was a beautiful strawberry blonde and I loved her with everything in my being.

"I thought we could watch it together, Granny." She looked at me speculatively.

"You haven't seen it already, have you?" she asked anxiously.

"No, dear."

I looked over the tops of my spectacles at Mary Honey, who knew my feelings on the subject.

She smiled with great innocence, knowing that I would now be forced to watch it.

"Pop and I are taking Auntie Agnes back to Kingston tomorrow night. Maybe you two could watch it then," she suggested. "The little girl who plays 'Anne' is Canadian. Your friend Lucy Maud would have approved of that, I'm sure. I think that the girl was actually born in Toronto."

I hated to admit it but I was glad of this information. At least it wouldn't be an American girl to play the heroine who was so distinctly Canadian.

"Aggie might like to watch it too," I said, turning to my sister.

"No," she said decisively. "Anne was always your thing. Olivia's the red-head; she should like it."

I saw no connection to this whatsoever, but like so many of Aggie's comments I let them float into the open air and dissolve there. Hank was providing her with a ride as her car had ended up in the shop the day before Christmas and we could not entertain the idea of her not attending the old farm for Christmas, crusty old school teacher that she was.

And so it was that Olivia and I had many hours to nestle in with our pillows and blankets and watch the entire two-pack video of Sullivan's production.

And I loved it. I loved the whole three hours and fifteen minutes of it. Olivia snuggled up beside me and we both fell in love. I could have rewound it and watched it right away again even as the closing credits were filling the TV screen.

I loved the little red-headed Megan Follows who was born in Toronto. I loved Colleen Dewhurst who played an austere but loving Marilla. But most of all I loved Richard Farnsworth as Matthew. I thought that if Lucy Maud could have seen Matthew in her mind and fashioned him into reality that he would have been this man. He was every farming man that I'd ever known: of the earth, kind, simple and good. When Matthew died out in the fields with Anne beside him, Olivia and I both dissolved into tears and clung to each other. I was hooked.

And so every single year Olivia and I make a date and watch our beloved movie together, because she grew to love the whole story just as I do. I have my very own red-head to watch my special story with at Christmas while the fabric Anne created by Mama so many years ago sits on my tree.

Quite recently I read in the paper that Richard Farnsworth had developed cancer which had metastasized, and he had taken his own life because of this. But every year at my house, even still, he becomes that kind elderly man who lies down in the red earth of his Prince Edward Island farm with his girl beside him and breathes his last. I don't cry much these days. I'm old. I'm all cried out. But that scene always finds Livy and me wiping our tears away. It's a tradition now.

I love having a granddaughter.

Olivia was eight years old, almost nine, on Christmas Eve 1987.

She made Christmas for us all. I always harbored wishes in my heart for more grandchildren, but that was not to be for Hank and me. It wasn't because we weren't thrilled with Olivia that I longed for more, but I had hoped for years that Mary Honey would find a new love and have more children.

She had so much love in her heart. But there existed in her heart as well a splinter of ice that had never quite melted since her brief and empty marriage and divorce. She always avowed that she was quite happy with Olivia and found her teaching career very rewarding. Agnes, of course, understood this. She, however, had never been married or had any children, so she didn't know the infinite joy that accompanied them. Hank and I would have had a dozen if the Lord had sent them, and I would have welcomed as many grandchildren.

But we only ever had our Livy–little red-headed Livy, who filled our homes and hearts with energy and love.

And so it was a shock, to put it mildly, when she remarked quite thoughtfully on this, her eight-year-old Christmas, that she wasn't absolutely sure about the "whole Santa Claus thing."

I felt myself taking a sharp intake of breath and looked at Hank. I don't quite know why I did, as men never know what to do in moments like this.

I sat down beside her and said very gently, "I'll tell you what my mama told me about Santa."

"What's that, Granny?"

"She used to say that Santa was the spirit of Christmas–that he signified all of the good things, caring and loving and helping others and giving to folk in need."

"She did, too." Agnes smiled at me. "I'd forgotten that she said that, but you're right, she did. The spirit of Christmas."

"I don't get it. I mean I know what a spirit is, but I don't see how that proves anything." Olivia was being a little perverse but I could see that she wanted something from us. I wanted so much to have the answers for her, but even now I didn't know them all myself.

"Wasn't that Virginia girl about your age when she asked the same question?" Hank turned to Agnes inquiringly.

"Virginia girl?" I was thinking locally and shrugged my shoulders without comprehension.

Olivia looked puzzled as well, but Agnes and Mary Honey were nodding slowly.

"Of course, Pops. You're right. She was eight years old–exactly eight years old.

You know, Mom. That famous article in the *New York Sun*. It was written back in the late 1890s or something and was reprinted every year until the paper closed down."

"Francis Church." Agnes was not to be left out of this important conversation.

"Who, Auntie Agnes?" Olivia looked puzzled.

"That's who wrote it. It was in response to an eight-year-old girl's letter to the editor. She tells him that some of her friends say there is no Santa and her papa tells her that if she sees it in the *New York Sun* then it must be true. So she asks the editor to tell her the truth. The editor's name was Francis Church."

"I actually have a copy of that editorial," Mary Honey was bustling around looking in her book bag. "I read it to my class every year."

"How come I've never heard it?" Olivia asked giving her mother a rueful look.

Mary Honey took her bright head between her hands and gave it a huge kiss right in the middle.

"Would you like to hear it now?" she smiled.

"I would," Hank said unexpectedly. "I haven't heard it since I was a boy. Somehow your mama missed that one, Hannah."

"Too busy looking up useless other facts like how long did the Grinch puzzle until his puzzler got sore," Agnes said with a grin that took the sting out of her words.

"Three hours!"

Everyone knew that one.

"Can you read it, Mom? I still like to hear you read things." Olivia perched beside her mom and we all fell silent.

It's such an old, old piece of literature and I suppose this is and will always be part of its charm. I am going to repeat it here in my little Christmas book because it is so beloved and because it is such a part of Christmas.

I was like Olivia. I loved to hear Mary Honey read in her soft, clear voice. Even Agnes was appreciative.

"Virginia, your little friends are wrong. They have been affected by the skepticism of a skeptical age. They do not believe except what they see. They think that nothing can be which is not comprehensible by their little minds. All minds, Virginia, whether they be men's or children's' are little. In this great universe of ours man is a mere insect. An ant, in his intellect, as compared with the boundless world about him, as measured by the intelligence capable of grasping the whole of truth and knowledge.

Yes, Virginia, there is a Santa Claus. He exists as certainly as love and generosity and devotion exist, and you know that they abound and give to your life its highest beauty and joy. Alas! how dreary would be the world if there was no Santa Claus. It would be as dreary as if there were no Virginias. There would be no childlike faith then, no poetry, no romance to make tolerable this existence. We should have no enjoyment, except in sense and sight. The eternal light with which childhood fills the world would be extinguished.

Not believe in Santa Claus! You might as well not believe in fairies! You might get your papa to hire men to watch in all the chimneys on Christmas Eve to catch Santa Claus, but even if they did not see Santa Claus coming down, what would that prove? Nobody sees Santa Claus, but that is no sign that there is no Santa Claus. The most real things in the world are those that neither children nor men can see. Did you ever see fairies dancing on the lawn? Of course not, but that's no proof that they are not there.

Nobody can conceive or imagine all the wonders there are unseen and unseeable in the world.

You may tear apart the baby's rattle and see what makes the noise inside, but there is a veil covering the unseen world which not the strongest man, nor even the united strength of all the strongest men that ever lived, could tear apart. Only faith, fancy, poetry, love, romance can push aside that curtain and view and picture the supernal beauty and glory beyond. Is it all real? Ah, Virginia, in all this world there is nothing else real and abiding.

No Santa Claus! Thank God! He lives and he lives forever. A thousand years from now, Olivia, *nay, ten times ten thousand years from now, he will continue to make glad the heart of childhood."*

Silence fell for a few moments.

"That was nice, Mary Honey." Hank said. "Thank you. I remember my mom reading that a long time ago."

"It's very old," Mary Honey agreed and smiled at her dad. "Like you, Pops."

"How true."

"Mom, did it really say Olivia at the end or did you put my name in?"

"I put your name in." Mary Honey told her daughter gently. "But it could have been written to any little girl really, even though it was a long time ago."

"Funny how he describes the 1890s as a skeptical age," Agnes mused. "Good reading, Mary Honey." Agnes added this as if Mary Honey were a schoolchild instead of a grown woman quite accustomed to reading in the classroom.

"I loved it too, Mom." Olivia hugged her mom and Mary Honey smiled tenderly at her.

"Does it answer your questions, my love?" she asked her tenderly.

"I think so," She looked at me and grinned. "It's like Granny says, I guess. He's the spirit of Christmas. Do you think that's what that guy means?"

I chuckled thinking that I had summed up a lengthy piece of literature in Mama's few words.

"Something like that," I agreed.

"I think that she was the spirit of Christmas," Mary Honey mused.

"Who?"

"Grandma. She's the one who made it so special all those years, even when we were sad she never gave up on it, did she?"

"No indeed," I agreed.

"She would like that," Agnes agreed. "She would like to be our Christmas spirit."

"Or maybe more like a Christmas angel," Mary Honey went on. "She seems so much a part of our Christmases even now."

Agnes and I laughed together.

"That's because she made so many things on the tree and so many decorations that we put out every year. And she was the Christmas champion of facts, that's for sure."

Later, much later after the annual trek out to light the candle and after all the lights were out for the night except for the gentle glow of the Christmas tree lights, I smiled softly to myself in the darkness. I fancied I could feel Mama's spirit close to me, as she'd always been close to me, my whole life.

The spirit of Christmas–Santa Claus and Mama–how could I go wrong?

In December of 1989 there occurred the horrific, senseless shooting of fourteen young engineering students in Montreal. I have nothing on my tree to represent this, but I think of them every year around this time.

It was a Canadian tragedy that is remembered each year, and each year my heart aches for the families of those girls who died so early in life, like my Danny, before life had even had a chance. I knew what it was like to lose someone at this time of year. It seemed worse somehow–the carols, the lights, the Santas–it seemed like a sacrilege.

Agnes was devastated by the occurrence. She was a teacher, a career woman, probably a feminist by definition. The deaths of those students went straight to her heart.

She was promoting, always, higher education for women and following your heart to your goals. This is quite the norm in present day, but when Aggie and I were growing up it was not a given as it is these days. We were lucky that Mama and even Dad felt that we should go to school as long as we wished and become what we desired in life. When we were young, more parents than not, especially farming ones, felt that education was just a necessity. My path did not take me very far away at all but that was entirely my own wishes. I was content at my own back door and never really wanted to stray too far. Agnes loved her career and was very successful as a teacher and later a principal.

"No wonder," Hank would joke with me, "It's not worth the aggravation of arguing with her. It's always so much easier to just agree."

"How well you know my sister."

We laughed together but it was completely and utterly without malice. We both loved Agnes dearly. She had dozens of good qualities and was as straight as an arrow. She was also the most opinionated woman I've ever known.

That self-assured woman was uncharacteristically quiet during her 1989 visit. Her smile was sad and strained. She was tender with ten-year-old Olivia and spent more than the usual amount of time with her.

"Has Granny got you schooled in the ways of Christmas yet, Livy dear?"

Olivia cocked her head in puzzlement.

"Oh, you know all of those Christmas facts that she parades around every year." Aggies smiled ruefully.

"I'm not like Mama," I admitted ruefully. "I wish I were."

"There's really nobody like her," Agnes agreed. She turned to her great niece and gave her a hug. "She would have loved you, little one."

"That's what my mom always tells me," agreed Olivia.

"It's true." I sighed and flung my tea towel over my shoulder, its usual place. "She would have just eaten you up."

"She sure did love this time of year," Agnes said. "She knew all about it. You could ask her anything–to this day I don't know how she did it."

"She would ask things like 'what does finding a spider web on Christmas morning mean?' She would always know little things like that," I said slyly.

Agnes turned an inquiring face towards me, but Mary Honey was getting into the swing of things.

"It means good luck," she avowed.

"What does?" Agnes asked.

"Finding a spider's web on Christmas morning," Mary Honey and I said in unison and in the exact tone of voice which made us all dissolve into laughter.

"If you actually got a gift for all of the twelve days of Christmas how many gifts would you have?" Mary Honey asked, getting into the spirit now.

Agnes looked at us and shook her head to signify that she had no idea.

"364." Again the answer came from me and Mary Honey.

Agnes was unconvinced and took to her pen and paper. Being a teacher she had to have things proven to her before she believed them. Even then there was no guarantee.

She looked up after a few moments and said that she thought there must be 78 and she had no idea where we got the number 364.

"But it's true, Aggie," I declared. "It is 364. I remember because Mama said that it was a gift for every day of the year minus one."

"Well this time Mama was wrong." Agnes seemed almost glad to win over a dead person.

Mary Honey, who had always been on Mama's side in life, did not falter now. After all, Mary Honey was also a school teacher and so knew fine well when she was right.

"Auntie Agnes, you are probably adding up 1,2,3,4,5,6,7,8,9,10,11 and 12 to get 78, aren't you? It's a common mistake."

Agnes had to admit that indeed she was. How else did it work?

"Well, you have to add up the consecutive gifts for each day."

"You've lost me," Agnes said.

Hank and I were lost as well but had no intention of admitting to this.

Mary Honey went into her classroom mode and started explaining.

"You see-day one you get one gift.

Day two you receive three additional gifts making a total of four.

Day three you receive six additional gifts making a total of ten.

Day four you receive ten additional gifts which makes a total of twenty.

Day five you receive fifteen additional gifts which makes a total of thirty-five–"

Mary Honey was writing this down methodically as she related it, but Agnes was nodding now.

"I get it. I get it. You're right, Mary Honey."

"Oh you may as well finish now," Hank egged her on. "You've only seven more."

By now Agnes had pen to paper as well and the rest of the song was done between the two women. Hank and I and Livy just chuckled and listened.

"Day six you receive twenty-one additional gifts making a total of fifty-six.

Day seven you receive twenty-eight additional gifts making a total of eighty-four.

Day eight you receive thirty-six additional gifts making a total of one-hundred and twenty.

Day nine you receive forty-five additional gifts making a total of one-hundred and sixty-five.

Day ten you receive fifty-five additional gifts making a total of two-hundred and twenty.

Day eleven you receive sixty-six additional gifts making a total of two-hundred and eighty-six.

And day twelve you receive seventy-eight additional gifts making a total of–"

"THREE-HUNDRED AND SIXTY-FOUR!"

The last number was said by all of us in the room, even ten-year-old Olivia.

It was a light moment in what was for my sister a dark Christmas season. She didn't mope around or include others in her sadness. That was not her way. But I was her sister, her one and only sibling. I could feel the sadness in her.

She spoke of this to me as we walked down the long lane on Christmas Eve to leave our beacon for the holy night. There was less and less snow with each passing year which is a fact that I chose to totally ignore and pretend wasn't true. I loved snow.

"That man–that horrible man."

I turned to look at her in the darkness.

"That Marc Lepine!" She said in a despairing voice.

"I knew who you meant, Agnes," I said gently and linked my arm in hers. We were walking a little behind Hank and Mary Honey and Livy. I pulled her to me in an embrace.

She started to sob.

"Oh Hannah, I just can't imagine those poor, poor families. They must have worked so hard to send those girls to university and then to have them shot down–fourteen of them, Hannah!"

"I know, dear. It doesn't bear thinking about. We'll never know why."

"No! Because the cowardly bastard shot himself too! Oh my God, Hannah! He just went into that classroom with a rifle and asked the men to leave and shot them–fourteen of them! Just because he thought they were feminists!"

I had no words of understanding to give my poor sister–only words of comfort on that cold winter night.

We did not know this at the time but some good did come out of that horrible tragedy, if indeed "good" it could be called. Governments tried to respond to make the public more aware of violence against women. Many institutions, one of which is Toronto's Women's College Hospital, hold annual memorial services, and in 1991 Parliament designated December 6th as an annual National Day of Remembrance and Action on Violence against Women. People became more aware of violence against women in general, and the age of sexual consent was raised from fourteen to sixteen.

Agnes and I kept our arms linked, by mutual consent, as we proceeded down the lane to catch up with the others and light our Christmas candle, our beacon in the big, bad world.

"Do you know what one of the other teachers said to me before the Christmas break?"

"What, Aggie?"

She said that her mom used to have a saying: 'God gave us memories so that we might have roses in December.' That's nice, isn't it, Hannah? We've got lots of roses, you and I, don't you think?"

"Yes, I do. And it is December."

"They were talking about the December of our *lives*, you know." Agnes took everything literally.

I felt a rush of affection for my sister so intense that it took my breath away for a moment. I turned to her. She was clad in her same old navy coat with her same old hat and mitts that Mama had knit for her a hundred years ago it seemed. I loved her. She was my sister.

"Agnes?"

"Hannah?"

She turned to me inquiringly.

"Thanks for always coming home and spending Christmas with us. It just would never be the same without you.'

And I meant it. I meant it forever.

She looked at me and seemed bewildered.

"Well where else would I be, Hannah? Where on earth would I be?"

Where, indeed?

Christmas 1992

The years were flying by as I counted them by the branches of my tree.

The threaded bulb that depicted 1992 had a baseball stamp on it and the famous Blue Jays logo.

I wasn't an avid sports fan by any means. The most excited I became was watching Olivia playing on her own little baseball team. Then I was absolutely sure who I was cheering for and did so with great enthusiasm.

The Blue Jays, however, were definitely in the limelight in 1992. They had been our Toronto team for fifteen years and had been unremarkable but I approved of them being Canadian, of course. People were very eager to point out to me that there were few if any actual Canadians on the team but I decided to like them because they represented our country.

October 24th of that fair year was to find Hank and Mary Honey yelling quite uproariously at the television set and screaming indeed with delight when our team won against the Atlanta Braves.

I could hear the songs erupting at regular intervals:

"We're not sure about Mulroney

But we all know Cito Gaston's right.
Come on, Jays!
Bring the world to TO!"
And snatches of the chorus
"OK Blue Jays
Let's-play-ball!"
This could be heard all over the house.

It was a great Canadian victory and everyone was in good spirits.

Dad, of course, was not living then but I thought of how I could have ribbed him about his precious Leafs. They had not won a Stanley Cup since 1967. I would only have been ribbing him, though. I was myself a Leafs fan. It was only fair to be loyal to your dad.

And they might win yet. I smile to myself as I rock my sweet great-granddaughter.

"Maybe in your time, Baby Hannah. Then again, maybe not."

And so it was not too surprising that a token of that great win had to be represented on my tree. I'm not certain who bought the ball. It might have even been Hank who usually left all of such things up to me entirely. But stranger things had happened. And after all, if you can find a Cabbage Patch Kid when no one else could, you could certainly find a Blue Jays ornament. They were most plentiful that year.

But that year is always bittersweet in my memory because 1992 turned out to be so much more than a baseball victory ornament. Especially to Olivia and me.

Olivia and I had an experience in December of that year which turned out to be unforgettable for both of us.

We had been to the cinema in Georgetown to watch *Home Alone Two: Lost in New York*. We had seen the first one two years ago when it was released, and we both loved it. We had all laughed and laughed as the robbers slowly were taken down at the mercy of an eight-year-old.

I liked that the sequel had the same cast of characters right down to every family member and even the same music. Olivia and I had loved it. We were bantering good naturedly on the way home if we liked it better than the first one, not usual in a sequel. But this time I thought that I really might prefer number two. I particularly liked the bird lady in the park and Olivia liked the antics of the hotel staff.

She was just quoting, between giggles,

"What kind of idiots do you have working here?"

"The finest in New York." We screamed with laughter as we quoted the line together. I was driving through Norval and I slowed down to look at the beautiful crèche in front of the United Church.

I loved that church so much. I didn't go every single Sunday but I did attend and I could feel Mama there. She sang in the choir for years and years and I could feel her presence strongly as I sat in the old worn pew.

"Look, Granny! That nativity is so sweet! Can you pull over so I can get a better look at it?"

I pulled over and put my head back on the seat of the car. It had been a busy day. I had done some shopping in Brampton. It used to be a rather small town but was rapidly growing and I found it quite tiresome to manoevour around its enormous malls these days.

Olivia leapt from the car and skipped over to the nativity which was lit up with a blue spotlight. She never ran out of energy, that kid, I thought ruefully.

"Granny!"

Olivia's ear splitting scream pierced to the interior of my little car. I hastened to pull open the door to see Olivia standing beside the crèche. She was illuminated in a beautiful blue light. I couldn't see anything out of the ordinary, but I got out of the car and stumbled over to her in the night air.

"Granny! Granny!" She was sobbing now and she held her face in her hands. I could hear her gasps and sobs through her trembling fingers. I was still mystified.

I approached her gently, wondering if she was having some sort of a seizure or something and put my hand on her shoulder.

"Olivia, darling! What on earth is the matter?"

I was, of course, totally focusing on my granddaughter.

She lifted her beautiful, innocent face to me and said, through a veil of falling tears, "Look, Granny, look."

She pointed at the crèche, more specifically the crude wooden manger which was the central focus of the whole scene.

I gasped.

There was a baby–a real, human baby-in the manger. It was all wrapped up in heavy blankets and would not have been visible from the road. But it was definitely a living, breathing baby.

"Granny–is he alive?"

Olivia's words were choked as she looked to me for guidance–guidance which I felt that I was sorely in need of myself. This was before everybody had a cell phone or a blackberry. There was no public phone box close by. I didn't know what to do.

I looked down at the baby and prayed with all of my might that this baby was indeed alive. I didn't think that I'd ever be able to look at Olivia's face again if he wasn't.

It took every scrap of courage I possessed to reach down and touch his cheek.

It was warm. I sobbed aloud with relief.

"He's alive, Olivia."

She exhaled sharply and sobbed anew. Together we picked the little bundle out of the manger and carried him over to our car which was still idling on the side of the road.

We put him down on the seat between us and carefully undid the blanket to look at his whole body.

He began to cry then. His little face screwed up as he wailed.

He was probably too cold to cry before, I thought to myself. This thought made me break into tears, too. Poor, poor child abandoned on a harsh December night outside in all of the elements.

"Oh you wee thing." I picked him up and hugged him to my breast. At least I was warm.

"He's soaked, Granny. Can we change him?"

"I have no diapers in the car."

And hadn't for quite some time.

"But there's a towel back here that you used to bring some buns to Mrs. Wilson's yesterday. At least he'd be dry."

I was glad that I wasn't a neat freak, I thought. I had a clean warm terrycloth towel to wrap around a soaking new baby's' bum.

And that's when we got our second shock of the night. It was on a much lesser scale than the first one, but it was still a shock.

"Why, Granny–it's a girl."

Indeed it was a little girl. A perfect baby girl with ten fingers and ten toes and as far as I knew not very many hours old at all.

"So she's really not Baby Jesus," Olivia declared.

I looked at her and felt totally unequal to the situation. Olivia was thirteen years old. Surely she must know that this was a flesh and blood baby and what it signified. Because if she didn't, I had nothing to offer. I was too overwhelmed with the magnitude of the whole thing.

She sensed my feelings and hastened to reassure me.

"Don't worry, Granny. I know that she's a real baby. I'm sorry. I guess I just thought she must be a boy because she was in the manger. You know?"

"I guess so, honey."

"Granny, look! There's a little holly decoration fastened here on her blanket."

"Yes, maybe her mommy put it there."

But where indeed was her mommy? I silently asked the cold December night sky.

"Her name must be Holly. Let's call her Holly."

"We can call her Holly if you like, but we have to find someone to look after her."

"Oh but Granny, we can look after her. We can take her back to the farm."

"No, sweetheart. We have nothing to feed her at home. She needs formula and bottles and medical attention."

"Is she sick?"

"No but she's very new, Olivia. She's only a few hours old, I think."

"But where's her mommy?"

Where, indeed?

"I have no idea. We'll take her to Georgetown Hospital. The nurses are really nice there. Remember when you got hurt at school and they were all so nice to you? We'll take Holly there."

Olivia was unconvinced. If she could have plucked that baby right out of the manger that night so long ago and kept her I'm quite sure that she would have. But instead I turned the car around and headed back to the hospital in Georgetown.

I suppose there was some law about infant seats by then. I didn't know and frankly at that moment I didn't care. We just wrapped that child up as warm and tight as we could and Olivia held her on her lap the whole way to the emergency department. I would have gladly been stopped by a policeman. But that didn't happen. I drove very slowly and carefully.

Olivia held the baby and spoke softly to her and kissed her little newborn face. I could scarcely drive for the tears streaming from my eyes.

It wasn't a very long drive–only five miles or so–but the whole trip was something that we never, ever forgot. It became a tangible thing for Olivia and for me to remember forever after.

As soon as we arrived at the hospital the staff went into their efficient roles and Baby Holly was whisked from us. Olivia and I sat in the waiting room as they took immediate care of her.

Then came the endless rounds of questioning. The police were called in and we had to tell our story many times and answer many questions. Most of these we had no answers for, and we repeated this time after time. I was completely and utterly spent.

At close to midnight a young, earnest doctor came out to the waiting room and sat beside us on the bench.

"The baby is going to be all right." He told us in a voice which was glad but weary. "You saved her life."

"It was Olivia. She found her."

"Well, Olivia, you did a very good thing today. A very important thing. You saved a life. Some people go their whole life and never get to do that. You are a hero, really."

"Thank you, Doctor," I whispered to him. What a kind young man to take the time to speak with a child so late in the night when he is obviously so busy.

"What will happen to her?" Olivia could not keep the tears out of her voice. She had taken Baby Holly straight into her heart.

"We will try very hard to find her mother. If we can't she will be adopted by a family who want a little baby girl so badly that they have been on a waiting list for years just in the hopes that they will get one."

Olivia sighed.

"That won't be like her very own mommy, though, will it?"

"No." he admitted honestly. "I can't promise you where she'll end up, but I can promise you that I will not let her leave the hospital until I'm sure that she has a very good home to go to."

"Please, can I see her just once more?"

"Why?" he asked not unkindly.

"I want to say goodbye to her."

He considered her earnest face for a moment and then he nodded his head in assent.

"Come with me."

I followed quietly behind them down the stark corridor to the warm cheerful nursery where a nurse sat in a corner with a bottle and a baby all bundled up rocking away contentedly. The nurse was older and looked tired but her careworn face was kind as she gazed at the cozy child.

The doctor explained our situation and she looked at us curiously.

"Thank God you stopped tonight." She spoke with a slight Irish accent.

"Olivia is the one who found her." I told her.

"Well thank God for you," she turned to Olivia. "You did a wonderful thing. You saved this baby's life."

"But why did her mommy leave her? Why?" Olivia was way past the point of exhaustion and her words were tearful.

The nurse said carefully, "We don't know that, dear, and we'll likely never know, to be sure. But I'll tell you one thing for certain."

Olivia waited expectantly.

"Her mommy loved her a lot."

"Really?"

"Really, my sweet. This baby has been fed and has been wrapped up in so many layers that I'm sure she was loved a lot. Maybe her mommy just couldn't keep her. It happens. You're a big enough girl to know that it happens sometimes, to be sure. And so it's our job–the doctors and nurses here–to give her to a home that loves her a lot."

"Can you do that?"

"We sure can. It's one of our specialties. There is a long, long list of lovely folk who are just waiting at home because they can't have their own baby and want one so badly."

"Can you make sure that Baby Holly goes to someone really, really nice?" Olivia asked softly.

The young doctor and the old nurse nodded solemnly and promised.

"And can you tell them that her name is Holly? See, she had a little holly leaf that somebody pinned to her inside blanket and I think they wanted her to have that name. It's so close to Christmas and it is a very nice name."

She looked at our small circle and we all agreed that indeed it was a great name, a lovely name.

"May I hold her one more time? Just in case I never see her again?"

The nurse rose and instructed Olivia to sit in the neat little rocking chair. Then she carefully placed Baby Holly in my sweet granddaughter's lap.

Olivia rocked her slowly and murmured to her. Tears were falling unchecked down her small cheeks.

"I will never, ever forget you, Baby Holly," she promised her. "You're going to go to a nice home and have a good family. But Granny and I will remember you forever."

She kissed the wee cheek that was warm now and smelled like clean linen and fresh milk.

"I'm all right now, Granny," she said, and we both sobbed as we made our way across the parking lot and headed home.

We never did forget Holly, Olivia and I. The others were of course touched by our experience, but I don't think that they really ever understood the magnitude or the effect that the whole experience had on Olivia and me. We were to carry her in our hearts forever.

I never did hear what happened to that infant, but I do have faith in the system which took her under its wing. Sometimes I think about where she is now and what she's doing, but in truth I don't even know what part of the world she exists in.

That year, as aforementioned, we hung a Blue Jays ball on the tree to represent 1992. There is another ornament that is found never too far from the baseball ornament. As if we could ever forget that year.

Several days before Christmas Mary Honey dropped in with Olivia and an ornament for my tree.

"I don't know what the hurry is," Mary Honey had been teaching all day and was obviously not in the mood for indulging silly whims. "But Livy insisted that we bring this out to you, Mom. She bought it herself and she wants you to hang it on your tree. I told her that I thought your tree is already so full that it might just keel over with all your stuff, but she insisted."

Hank was already pouring her a cup of tea and she was easing into the kitchen chair, allowing Olivia to present me with a round gaily wrapped ball.

It was a ball of holly with little feet and arms and a tiny head emerging from it.

I hugged her to me and we selected a branch to hang the ornament on.

"We'll never forget her," I promised her.

And we didn't of course.

How could we?

"What's the full name of Dickens Christmas book?"

Agnes was back in full Christmas form. I'm sure she boned up on plenty of research regarding all things Christmas so that she could produce her knowledge at intervals during the Yuletide season. Or so it seemed.

We took it in our stride, Hank and I and Mary Honey and Olivia. I think that she was somehow doing it for Mama but she didn't realize that Mama had done it with love. I wasn't sure what drove Aggie to these deep discussions but she seemed to enjoy them so we all did our best. Our best seemed quite poor to Agnes at times, I'm sure. But still we persevered.

"A Christmas Carol." I said promptly. "It's my favorite Christmas book, actually."

"Well, then Hannah you should know the full name of the book."

"It's 'A Christmas Carol in Prose; Being a Ghost Story of Christmas," Mary Honey came to my rescue with a grin. "That's right, isn't it, Auntie Agnes?"

"Oh yes, my dear that's right. Do you read it to your students?"

"Yes, parts of it. Not the whole book to be sure. I think everyone should read it through at least once, though. It's such a classic."

"I always felt kind of sorry for that poor old Ebenezer Scrooge," Hank piped up, more I'm sure to be the devil's advocate than for want of any Dickens discussion.

"Sorry for Scrooge? Why on earth, Pops? He was a miserable old man."

"Well, that's just exactly why. He didn't love anyone and no one loved him."

"It was his own fault."

"Yes, true but when he was young, he was left all alone at the school for Christmas break and his own father wouldn't let him come home until his sister begged and begged."

"But, Pops, that's the whole point of the story. He couldn't change the past. He could only observe it."

"Yes, I realize that my dear little school teacher. I'm just saying that it isn't easy to have no home. He didn't have a mother and his father didn't want him."

"We are taking the book very literally," Agnes said, in a voice that just missed being peevish.

"I thought that's what you wanted to do," I said. "And before you ask the question around the room I happen to know what year it was published and how much it sold for."

"Indeed."

"1843. And five shillings was the price."

"How much is that in real money?" Olivia asked.

"It was British currency." It was Agnes who was forthcoming with this knowledge. I had exhausted mine for now.

"I never really did understand their way of defining money. We are so much more straightforward."

"Does that mean you don't know, Auntie Agnes?"

We all laughed at this.

"A shilling is a bob, I think," Hank suggested.

"A bob?"

"That's a slang British term."

"But how much is it, Papa?"

"I think that a shilling is twelve pennies," Mary Honey said. "I think it's either that or one twentieth of a pound. And I think that the value of the pound would vary and so the value of the shilling would vary as well."

"Anyway," Olivia said, evidently tired of the whole money determination, "That's not very much money for a book, is it?"

"No, not by today's standards for sure. But don't forget that was one hundred and fifty years ago. There was not too much money around."

"I think that I read somewhere that he wanted the price to be only five shillings so that everyone would be able to afford a copy." Agnes continued. She was not finished displaying her Christmas knowledge.

"Well he must have been a nice man then, mustn't he, Auntie Agnes?" Olivia nodded with approval in her voice.

"I think that he must have been, dear."

"I like the old, old movie the best," Hank said. He turned to me. "You know, the one with that old fool with the spiky white hair."

"Oh, Alistair Sim. That is old, but I like it, too. I think it was probably the most like the actual book."

"True," Mary Honey agreed. "They've done a lot of remakes, but that one seems the most Dickens-ish."

"That's the one with the silly man who tries to stand on his head at the end because he's so happy. I've watched it a time or two with Papa. It's seriously old. It's not even color."

"Well I have to get it on the TV once in a while in between re-runs of Jimmy Stewart," Hank winked at me.

"Jimmy Stewart is much more handsome than that grouchy old crock, that's for sure. No contest there, Hank Moreau. I do like the old Christmas Carol too, though. None of these new versions seem to measure up."

"They are doing a reading of *A Christmas Carol* at one of the schools in Kingston,"

Agnes said.

"Is that why you've been looking it up? Are you a part of that reading?" I asked.

"No. I'm not."

"Well you should be," I continued. "You'd be good at it."

"Thanks, Hannah. Actually, I wasn't asked."

"Shows how much they know," Hank said. "You have a great reading voice. You should read it for us."

I was slightly horrified. The whole book!

"Not the whole book, of course," he continued, as if reading my mind. "But the ending. I love the ending, and it's great to hear it from someone who really knows how to read it."

"Well, thank you, Hank."

Agnes was clearly flattered. "I'll just read the last page, will I?"

She looked around our little group and we all nodded our assent.

She got out Mama's old, worn copy and announced that she would start on the day after Christmas when poor unsuspecting Bob Crachit came in apologizing for being tardy:

"It's only once a year, sir," pleaded Bob, appearing from the tank. "It shall not be repeated. I was making rather merry yesterday, sir."

"Now, I'll tell you what, my friend," said Scrooge. "I am not going to stand this sort of thing any longer. And therefore," he continued, leaping from his stool and giving Bob such a dig in the waistcoat that he staggered back into the tank again, "Therefore I am about to raise your salary!"

Bob trembled and got a little nearer to the ruler. He had a momentary idea of knocking Scrooge down with it, holding him and calling to the people in the court for help and a straight waistcoat.

"A Merry Christmas, Bob!" said Scrooge, with an earnestness that could not be mistaken, as he clapped him on the back. "A merrier Christmas, Bob, my good fellow, than I have given you for many a year! I'll raise your salary and endeavor to assist your struggling family, and we will discuss you affairs this very afternoon, over a Christmas bowl of smoking bishop, Bob! Make up the fires and buy another coal scuttle before you dot another I, Bob Cratchit!"

Scrooge was better than his word. He did it all, and infinitely more; and to Tiny Tim, who did not die, he was a second father. He became as good a friend, as good a master, and as good a man, as the good old city knew, or any other good old city, town or borough, in the good old world. Some people laughed to see the alteration in him, but he let them laugh, and little heeded them, for he was wise enough to know that nothing ever happens on this globe, for good, at which some people did not have their fill of laughter at the onset; and knowing that such as these would be blind anyway, he thought it quite as well that they should wrinkle up their eyes in grins, as have the malady in less attractive forms. His own heart laughed; and that was enough for him.

He had no further intercourse with Spirits, but lived upon the Total Abstinence Principle, ever afterward; and it was always said of him, that he knew how to keep Christmas well, if any man alive possessed the knowledge. May that be truly said of us, and all of us! And so, as Tiny Tim observed, God Bless Us, Every One!"

Agnes was a very good elocutionist and we were all touched by her reading.

"It's never lost any of its charm in all these years, has it?" I asked. "Well done, sis."

"For sure," Hank agreed.

"And God bless us every one!" Mary Honey said laughing and hugging her aunt.

"Peace on earth and good will among women!" Hank declared, grinning broadly.

We all laughed.

"When did you think that up, Papa?"

"You like that, Livy? I thought it up in my very own brain and I was just waiting to get a word in with all of you women to say it!"

Olivia was a great fan of Winnie the Pooh and growing into girlhood did not make her abandon that silly old bear at all. If anything, she liked him more. That was one of the things I always loved about Livy. She didn't care if it wasn't "cool" to like Anne Shirley or Winnie the Pooh or her grandparents. She just went right on liking them.

She was always quoting him as if he were an accurate frame of reference.

"Some people care too much. I think it's called love."

I never knew that Pooh was anything other than a bear who ate so much honey that he got stuck in a doorway and had to wait until he got smaller so that he could fit through. I thought that he was a very greedy fellow, to say the least.

But Livy laughed and told me that I just didn't understand him. If I did take the time she was sure I would just love him because he and I looked at things much the same way.

I didn't think so.

"Come on Granny! You love *Anne of Green Gables*."

"I certainly do. So do you."

"I sure do. I love her quotations. But you know, Granny, some of Pooh's are even more pertinent to everyday life."

I laughed and shook my head.

"Okay, Livy, if you say so. But *Anne of Green Gables* is literature, you know."

"So is Pooh Bear. A.A. Milne was a very renowned British author."

"Ah, Hannah, I think she's got you there," Hank chuckled lightly.

"I do. I do have Granny there, Papa. A.A Milne was very famous."

"He's dead, isn't he?"

"Yes, he died in 1958. But Lucy Maud is dead too."

"Look out, Hannah, sooner or later she's going to make you watch Winnie the Pooh at Christmas alongside your Anne movie."

"No, Papa. I don't expect Granny to watch the cartoons with me, but every time I find a great quote made by my fuzzy little friend I'm going to copy it out in nice fancy letters and tape it up on my bedroom walls."

"Your bedroom here?"

"Of course, silly. Mom wouldn't let me deface my room at home."

We all laughed then because Olivia's room here was an utter mish mash of everything imaginable. That was just how it was.

And so gradually Olivia's walls did become filled with quotations from the famous bear. They were all highlighted in various colors so we could define them easily.

The room upstairs at the end of the hall is still referred to as "Olivia's" room even today although that redheaded whirlwind does not grace it with her presence anymore, having long since grown up. But we've never removed her things from it.

When I dust it or sweep the floors it gives me indefinable pleasure to read her walls, and I'm glad that we allowed her to express herself in this way. Sometimes I would post little messages in between her papers and she loved that. She would sometimes enter it and scour the walls in search of my touch. But most of the messages were distinctly Olivia.

"When looking at your two paws as soon as you have decided which of them is the right one, then you can be sure that the other is your left."

After these lines I added, "I have that trouble with my hands at times."

"People who don't think probably don't have brains–rather they have gray fluff that's blown in their heads by mistake."

I thought that Olivia was beginning to leave a little space at the end of her quotes on purpose so that I could write something witty. This was not easy to do. I was not witty by nature. But I always made an attempt.

After this last quote, I wrote, "What was that, Miss Gray Fluff?"

"Very funny, Granny dear," was added after this.

"It's more fun to talk with someone who doesn't use long difficult words but short easy ones like 'what about lunch?'"

"That bear is always thinking of his stomach," I countered in my small handwriting.

"Promise me you'll always remember: you're braver than you believe, and stronger than you seem and smarter than you think."

I couldn't argue with this and I wrote to Olivia that this time Pooh Bear got it right on. She wrote back that it wasn't Pooh who said this but that it had been said to Pooh by Christopher Robin.

"I still agree with it," I wrote on the last little bit of the paper.

I laughed as I recalled the sheets of paper that still lined the wallpaper of Olivia's room upstairs. I had never taken them down. There remained that bit of history.

People talk back and forth on Facebook now and in emails. This was years before any of these things were prevalent. Our conversations lived forever on the pen and paper of the old bedroom walls.

"Isn't it nice to think that tomorrow is a whole new day without any mistakes in it yet???"

That was my contribution to the wall.

"Yes, indeed Granny. I haven't forgotten Anne, you know. I think that she'd have liked Pooh's sentiment, though."

"He had a sentiment?" I was running out of paper room and almost wrote on the wallpaper. But I crammed it in.

The next time when Livy came to stay over, there was a new sheet of foolscap up on the wall and ready for our running commentary.

"He did, Granny," she wrote. "You don't appreciate my fuzzy little friend, that's all."

"Humph!" was my firm reply but I dragged it out across the page until it looked quite impressive.

"Did you ever stop to think and forget to start again?" Of course these were Winnie's words.

"Of course I have," I countered her, on paper, "I'm old enough to be a grandmother to a saucy fifteen-year-old. So there!"

The funniest thing about this whole communication was that we never spoke of it. We just wrote it. It wasn't private. Anyone at all could have gone into that room at the top of the stairs and read what was clearly written on the walls–back and forth–in two distinct forms of handwriting. But no one did and that made it all the more hilarious.

"It didn't matter where they went as long as they went together. That's you and me, Granny."

"OK you've got me there." I wrote. "Do you want to go Christmas shopping, Livy dear?"

Of course, we did go Christmas shopping together. We went every year. We shopped well together, which is not as common a trait as one might imagine. But on the way home we ended up in the ditch just as we were turning onto our road. There was ice under a little skiff of snow and we fishtailed right off the beaten track. No damage was done, but we had to break down and call Hank to come with the old tractor. He hauled us out quite successfully and no one was the worse for wear.

But the next time Olivia slept over there was a new quote on the wall and I howled with laughter as I read it. She reminded me of Mama. She must research these things to death and then innocently put them into play when they were most appropriate.

"They're funny things, accidents. You never have them till you're having them."

I countered with an Anne quote: "After all what would you expect from a pig but a grunt?"

"Winnie the Pooh speaks," she wrote after this one. "'It's always useful to know where a friend and relation is whether you want him or whether you don't.' Like if you need pulling out of a ditch with your Christmas parcels."

"It's so much more friendly with two," I countered.

"Granny! You're quoting him now! I'm so impressed."

"Well, once in a while he does say something worthwhile," I admitted on the wall after this comment.

"Well, as Anne says, life is worth living as long as there's a laugh in it." Olivia had the last word on that particular page because as usual every inch was covered in writing.

That was the year when Olivia made me a Winnie the Pooh ornament with that silly old bear replicated by her own hand and the words encircling the whole thing saying, "A little consideration, a little thought for others makes all the difference."

I laughed when I saw it. Then I allowed myself to gaze meaningfully at the plaque I had found at Hallmark and hung up in my kitchen. Olivia followed my gaze and read the plaque with delight.

Who knew that Hallmark would be quoting Winnie as well as Olivia? I liked this one of his sayings the very best of all, though, and I understood it the best.

"If you live to be a hundred, I'd like to live to be a hundred less a day so that I never have to live a day without you."

I suppose everyone who loves a child feels that way.

Way to go, Winnie!

The new millennium came and the world kept on turning. The

ornament that I have for that year is a glowing royal blue bulb with gold etching and letters proclaiming,

"Norval United Church 1850-2000."

I loved it. Olivia had bought one for me and one for Agnes at the Montgomery celebration in Norval. They had started having this annually at the end of November to mark that great author's birthday. It was a great kick start to the festive season.

Upon receiving the Christmas ball, Agnes had taken me aside and said, "It's a nice sentiment and all, Hannah, but I never get a tree for my place. I always spend the holidays with you. Where on earth am I supposed to hang it?"

I chuckled to myself and shook my head. If Agnes didn't understand the gesture for more than a "nice sentiment" then I was unequal to the task of explaining it to her.

Nonetheless, she thanked Livy quite graciously as she accepted it.

I loved the shiny blue ball. It would always remind me of Mama. I knew, however, that for Olivia the little country church would always bring to mind the infant that we found there beneath the stars. It had been years ago now and Olivia was an adult, but I knew that Baby Holly lived on in her kind heart and always would.

She had started to take graphic design at Sheridan College but had recently done an about face and decided that she would like to be a nurse and specialize in pediatrics.

Mary Honey had been quite supportive of this, considering that Olivia's father had apparently fallen off the face of the earth and never produced a nickel of child support. She never said this aloud, however, and I was proud of her for that. At least she never said it aloud in Olivia's earshot. But Hank and I both knew that it was tough being a single parent, both emotionally and financially.

Surprisingly, though, it was Agnes who had stepped up to the plate at this point in Olivia's life. When discussions of tuition and books and college expenses in general were being tossed around and around the table, she surprised us all with a very generous offer.

She was all for education for everyone [being a teacher I guess she had to practice what she preached], but she particularly wanted women to get as much knowledge and learning as they possibly could.

"I have a lot of money in the bank, never having had any kith nor kin of my own–present company excepted, of course. And so I want Olivia to take it for her college expenses."

She said this in her usual clipped business like way and nodded her head as if to say that this was the end of it.

"Oh my, Auntie Agnes, we can't accept that," Mary Honey and Olivia were protesting as in one voice.

Agnes waved their protests away.

"Don't be silly, girl. What on earth am I going to do with my money if you don't use it? I don't have anyone to leave it to and it would give me great pleasure to pay for Livy's schooling while I'm still alive to see her make something of her life."

Being Agnes, she could not resist adding her opinion to her generous offer.

"Why you want to be a nurse, though, is beyond me–working shift work and night shifts and cleaning up unspeakable things."

She shuddered just thinking about it.

Olivia got up and hugged her great aunt.

"Thank you so much Auntie Agnes. I won't let you down, you know. And I want to work with babies. They don't do too many unspeakable things."

Agnes was unconvinced but a smile came over her stern features at Olivia's gratitude and pleasure.

Later as Livy helped me in the kitchen she took my hand and pulled me to her.

"Granny–*you* know why I want to work with babies, don't you? You understand."

I kissed her smooth cheek.

"Yes, dear I do. I think you will be a wonderful baby nurse. But I don't want you to feel badly about Holly anymore."

"I can't help it. I think about her so much and at Christmas I can't get her out of my mind. She would be a girl of eight now, but I can't help it. When I think of her she is always a little baby left out in the cold. Oh, Granny, I wanted to keep her so much!"

"I know, darling girl. I know. But she is better off now. The health care people wouldn't have let her go unless it was to a loving family."

"Do you believe that, Granny?"

"Yes, my dear. I believe it with my whole heart. Sometimes, Livy, you just have to have faith in things."

"Will you have faith for me if I just can't?"

"Always."

Olivia loved nursing but it was very hard work. I couldn't make head nor tail out of some of the huge text books which came to rest regularly on my kitchen table. She plugged away at them ceaselessly and tirelessly, so it seemed.

And then she met a boy.

That's how she told us.

"Granny! Papa! I met a boy."

"A boy?"

"Yes you know, Papa. A member of the opposite sex."

"Oh, one of those creatures."

"Yes, one of those creatures."

"Is he a special boy? I presume he must be if you're telling your old grandma and grandpa about him."

She flushed deeply.

Uh-oh! I thought. This could be serious. And why not? Olivia was into her twenties and as pretty as a picture with her clear blue eyes and strawberry blonde curls. It was unrealistic to think that we would keep her to ourselves forever. Tempting, but unrealistic.

"He is special, yes. I was thinking that you might like to meet him."

"Has your mom met him yet?"

"No. I was hoping that you could all meet him together."

"Get it all over with at the same time, sort of?"

"Papa!" Livy gave him a playful shove. "It's not like that. He goes to Sheridan with me and he's from up north. I thought that maybe I could ask him out for a meal some night and we could all get to know each other."

"Of course, you can, child. We'd love to meet him."

"You're quite sure of that are you, Hannah? That we'd love to meet him, I mean?"

"Papa, don't tease me. I'm trying to be serious."

"Sorry, Livy. Where did you say he's from?"

"Burkes Falls. It's just past Huntsville."

"Well, that isn't north you know. Did you forget that your old grandpa hails from Timmins?"

"I know that, Papa. But it *is* north of here."

Hank grinned and admitted that indeed it was.

And so we met Kevin. And we had to admit that he was special. He was big and burly and freckled with a face as round and open as the sun.

"Well, what did you think of the boy?"

Agnes phoned from Kingston that night for the news.

"We thought that he was very nice. Hank and I both liked him a lot. He is pleasant and well mannered. When Hank went outside to get some wood for the fire he just got up and went out to help him. He says that he chops wood with his father and brother in Burkes Falls, and so he's used to throwing it around. He's a big fellow–well over six feet."

"Well that's good. You never know nowadays. Some of the young people floating around are pretty dubious."

I laughed at my predictable sister.

"Well, he's not dubious, Aggie. He's just an ordinary nice young fellow. Oh, and he invited us–all of us–up to his parents' home for Thanksgiving dinner. I guess they make kind of a big deal of it–his mom does anyways."

"That's weeks away, for God's sake!"

"Oh, Aggie, do you not know how fast the weeks go by now? That can't just be me."

"I know how fast time goes for sure. But she may not even be going out with this fellow in October."

"She's quite smitten, I think."

Agnes harrumphed.

"You're invited too, you know."

She harrumphed again.

"He doesn't even know I exist."

"Not true, sister dear. He knows quite well that you exist and not because of me. Olivia must have been giving him the run down on all of us because when he invited us he included you. 'And don't forget about your Aunt Agnes.' His exact words."

"I don't know if I want to be called Aunt Agnes by a complete stranger."

I stifled a sigh. Sometimes there was just no pleasing my sister.

"You'll have to meet him, Aggie. I'm sure that when you do you'll like him. I hope so because I have a feeling that he's here to stay."

As it turned out Agnes did not accompany us on our first trip up to Burkes Falls, but she did get her very own personal invitation, which kept her satisfied–for a while anyways.

Hank and I had really not entertained any serious intention of driving all the way up there ourselves. We had always been perfectly happy to have our Thanksgiving dinner at home. Olivia and Kevin seemed to have their hearts set on us all attending, though.

Kevin said that his family loved Thanksgiving, especially his mom.

He told us of where they lived and how beautiful and isolated it was, and how the trees up there at this time of year were so awesome that they must be seen to be believed.

Hank gave in when he saw how much Olivia wanted us to go and they both seemed overjoyed at our decision. I was a little nervous but we said we'd go and go we did.

We had agreed before we realized that this was actually a two-day event–that is, a staying overnight event–a sleepover, in fact. We were to drive up on Saturday morning and stay overnight at the McDonalds' home in Burkes Falls. We were to have Thanksgiving supper in the early evening of Thanksgiving Sunday leaving us enough time to travel home in the daylight. Or we were quite welcome to stay another night until Monday, but that particular day could be very hectic on the highway with all of the cottagers driving home after the long weekend.

Mary Honey and Hank did not seem to mind this very much, but I had misgivings. I was almost seventy, and I had never been too much for travelling beyond my own comfort zone.

But I would have walked through fire and brimstone for Olivia, so I did my best to make an effort.

And I ended up enjoying every moment of our visit.

Kevin had been very casual about his parents, assuring me that they loved company and that they loved Olivia and his mom was Irish and adhered to the sentiment "the more the merrier."

I wondered if he was perhaps seeing her through rose colored glasses but I could see right away that she was indeed just as sweet and welcoming as her son had described.

I had been fussing a little in the car–just a little–as we were turning onto the Burkes Falls cutoff, and Hank had assured me that if they did not seem to really want us there that we could simply make some excuse and politely leave.

That did not prove to be necessary.

Caragh McDonald was small and dark with laughing brown eyes and a big smile. She came down the porch steps as our car entered their driveway and ran nimbly out to embrace her son. He was easily a whole foot taller than she was and she disappeared for a moment in his big arms. Then she hugged Olivia warmly and planted a kiss on her young cheek before turning to us with genuine pleasure in her face.

Introductions were made all around and then she hollered for her husband and son to get "out of the woodwork and meet their guests."

The men obliged, wiping their brows and then wiping their hands on their jeans after emerging from a copse of spruce trees.

More introductions were made–Kevin's brother Keith, who was big and sunny, too, and Neil, Kevin's father, who was quite small and wiry looking. It seemed impossible to think that this couple who were both quite small in stature could have achieved these two huge men.

"Come in! Come in! Sure and you're as welcome as the flowers in May, you are," Caragh put one arm through mine and one through Mary Honey's and we proceeded into the old fashioned kitchen where there was tea brewing and a cake cooling on the shelf. We proceeded to partake of both of these with great pleasure.

"My goodness this is good," Mary Honey commented, surveying her slab of cake.

"Ah, there's a secret ingredient in it, to be sure," Caragh winked at her.

"It's probably something sinful," Mary Honey observed dryly.

"Oh, maybe a wee bit sinful, that's all," Caragh admitted.

"Is that possible?" I asked with a grin.

"For sure." She laughed. "As my old grandma in Ireland used to say 'sin is like beauty–it's all in the eye of the beholder.'"

We all laughed.

"My granny once told me something like that," Mary Honey commented.

"She did?" I was surprised.

"Oh yes, Mom. Granny and I used to talk about all kinds of things. One day I was about seventeen and I was in a store with her. We were looking at posters and sayings on plaques and stuff, you know."

"Oh yes, I know about those kinds of sayings."

I winked at Olivia who still maintained a running commentary written across her bedroom walls at the old farmhouse. I wondered if Mary Honey even knew about this. It would make for amusing reading one fine day, that was for sure.

"Well, Granny was looking for a particular plaque, I can't even remember what it was now. But I do remember that the lady in the store pointed out a plaque with the Ten Commandments on it to see if she'd like that one instead. Granny and I looked at the plaque and I said to her that really I'd already broken some of them. Don't forget I was seventeen, and thought I was pretty darned smart. The lady in the store looked quite offended, but dear old Granny, do you know what she said?"

Mary Honey was looking at me now. I shook my head.

"Well, she patted my shoulder and said, 'Don't worry, Mary Honey. They're only a guideline.'"

Everyone laughed but I felt a rush of longing for Mama. I'd never heard that particular story, but it sounded so much like Mama that it struck a chord inside my heart. She had always given people their due for being the best they could be.

"We're only human," she was wont to say. "We are not expected to be anything more. That is up to God himself, after all."

Caragh leaned forward and patted my arm.

"That would be your mom?" she asked softly.

I smiled and nodded.

"I like the sounds of her." She said.

Okay, how could I not like this lady?

That Saturday afternoon the girls all took a little side trip into the nearby town of Huntsville to look around. I had driven past this picturesque town before but had never actually been inside of it.

I was surprised at how naturally Hank melted into the woods with Keith and Kevin and Neil McDonald. It's a man thing, I guess. They had logs, they had axes, and they had four-wheelers. Later on when these were all put away they had homemade beer.

It's a man thing, all right.

And shopping, of course, is a girl thing. I was absolutely delighted with the streets of Huntsville. I loved the little shops and the friendly people, a lot of whom waved a cheery hello to Caragh and even to the rest of us as we accompanied her along the way. I loved the way cars stopped in midstream to let you cross the street. I loved how the whole downtown was on a tilt, starting at the crest of a hill until you reached the bottom, where a bridge crossed the beautiful river that flowed beneath it.

But most of all–oh, most of all– there was a Christmas store at the bottom of that hill. Olivia's eyes were fairly snapping when we reached it, and she turned around so that I could read the sign: "Christmas Tyme."

"Granny, I can hardly wait to show you inside this store. You will just love it!"

I loved it already. There, on the front of the store, was a plaque proclaiming the sentiment: "I shall hold Christmas in my heart…and keep it all the year through." Charles Dickens.

There was also a chalkboard posted outside that looked like it kept a running tab of how many days until Christmas. The number written there today was 79.

When I walked inside I was mesmerized. There was Christmas music playing and trees and ornaments everywhere.

Caragh pointed out some round red balls hanging up on a separate wall. They had been personalized with different names

"He'll write anything that you like on these balls. They are quite legendary. Many people get one with the birth of a child or grandchild. Bob does all of the writing himself."

A dark haired man behind the countered smiled and waved.

"I'm Bob," he declared.

"You do an amazing job," I told him.

The blonde lady who was standing beside him smiled at me. "He wants all of the balls to have the same handwriting, you see. The girls and I–we are allowed to personalize the other ornaments but not those balls. They are sacred."

"I think that is admirable," I told him and they both laughed.

What a nice couple, I thought, and how appropriate that they own a Christmas store.

Mary Honey wanted to look at a bookstore further down the street, and so Caragh offered to take her as it was evident that I was not done exploring this extraordinary place.

Olivia stayed behind with me and we exclaimed together over this one and that one. Some were funny ["Dear Santa, Leave presents take brother/sister" or "Mom loves ME the best"] and some were particular to hobbies and professions but most of them were just unique and amazing. I had never been in a store even remotely like this one. I picked out an ornament that I wished to leave for Caragh and Neil as a small token of our appreciation for their kindness. It had a picture of an old fashioned house on the front of it and the year.

Bob asked me if I wanted it personalized. I hadn't realized that this was possible.

"Oh, we can personalize anything," he assured me with a smile, and picked up his special tipped pen.

After much debating I decide on a message and he wrote simply, 'Thank you for your hospitality.'

"I think that says what you want it to say quite nicely," he told me.

I was not to know this at the time, but this was to become a yearly tradition–the trip to Burkes Falls, the side trip to Christmas Tyme, and the selection of an ornament for the McDonald family.

He wrapped it up and put it in a bag, which is when I noted that the quote from Dickens was on the bottom of the paper bags as well.

"I love that you included this," I told them. "It's a great quote."

"My grandma is all about Christmas," Olivia explained to this Christmas store couple.

"Oh, that's wonderful," The girl said. "We love it, too–well, obviously."

She was blonde and attractive and I learned that her name was Tracey.

"It was actually my own mom who started it," I said and then, because they really seemed genuinely interested, I told them a little about Mama.

Olivia took up the conversation thread, talking about some of the old ornaments that I have cherished lovingly dating back to my own 1935 baby ornament and Anne Frank and Jimmy Stewart. The store had been steady with customers earlier but there seemed to be a lull just now, and so we continued our chatter as we waited for Caragh and Mary Honey.

Behind the counter there was a wreath with holly leaves intertwined into a circle and the letters "Holly for Sale" inserted in the center. My eye caught it, I think, just at the same time that Livy's did and, startled, we looked at each other.

"What is it? Is something the matter?" Tracey asked kindly.

"Oh, no," I assured her. "Everything is fine."

But the couple were looking at Olivia uncertainly.

I don't know if she was feeling emotional about being in Kevin's town or because we were talking about Christmas Past or just because these people were certainly people who knew how to "keep

Christmas well," and were obviously sympathetic. Or maybe it was just that it was time to tell Holly's story.

Whatever the reason, Olivia told them all about finding Holly in the dark of that winter's night, in that crude, rugged manger. She told of saving her, only to lose her again to the social system. When she was finished she stumbled out of the store, overwhelmed with emotion.

That kind couple stood there with great compassion on their young faces, shaking their heads in wonder that such a thing could happen.

"I've never known her to talk about that night much at all, even to me. She doesn't tell many people about it. Thank you for listening."

"My, what a great impression that must have made on such a young girl. How old did you say she was at the time?"

"She was only thirteen. There was just she and I and we were both absolutely petrified. At first I didn't know if the baby was even alive, and then I just couldn't believe that anyone would abandon her. That is the part that haunts Livy, I think."

"It's too bad that somehow she couldn't have known for sure the baby went to a good home."

"I have thought that often, but I tell her that for some parts of our lives we just have to have faith and be content with that."

They both nodded. We were silent, all of us thinking about Baby Holly.

Olivia came back into the store in a few moments, fully composed.

"I'm sorry. I haven't told anyone else that story since I was thirteen years old. I haven't even told Kevin yet. I hate getting weepy and all that. But you are Christmas people and I felt that I could tell you."

"Don't apologize. I'm glad you felt you could tell us that story. We won't forget about Baby Holly. It's a wonderful story really, you know. They might have found that baby in the morning and the whole story would have a different ending. I think that you were called upon to be a Christmas angel that night."

"Yes, and a very fine Christmas angel at that," her husband agreed.

"Thank you. It's my granny who is actually the Christmas angel. I told you about her ornaments, but she has lots of stories and little Christmas things that she knows to go along with it all."

"You should write a little Christmas book," Bob suggested.

I scoffed at the idea.

"Sure and what would it be? Just a list of decorations on an ancient old pine tree?"

"Oh, Granny! It would be so much more than that," Olivia declared.

It was at this point in time that the other two returned from their trip to the bookstore with several new packages.

"Enough about Christmas for now," Caragh declared with a laugh. "Let's go and celebrate Thanksgiving!"

When we returned to the family home in Burkes Falls, the men were coming out from the bush and Neil McDonald and Hank–my Hank!–were singing together these lyrics:

"Ah dee doo–ah dee doo-ah dee day

Ah dee doo-ah dee day o-o-oh!

He whistled and he sang till the green woods rang

And he won the heart of a la-a-ady!"

"Oh my God–how much has Pops had to drink?" Mary Honey exclaimed.

"Oh they're fine," Caragh assured her. "It's just a little homemade brew that Neil has from time to time."

"Pops really isn't used to too much liquor, though," Mary Honey worried.

But Caragh was right. They really were fine, just being loud and boisterous as men are when they're together. One would think that a man of almost seventy would be too old to partake of such activities but apparently some things are timeless.

It was all very different from our everyday life. Still, Hank and I enjoyed ourselves immensely, much to our own surprise. It was a beautiful autumn day and the trees were magnificent in their color and splendor. We sat on the porch and talked and later came inside and played euchre. Hank and I were both a little rusty, but we sharpened up as the evening wore on.

At one point Olivia and Kevin went out for a walk and Caragh and Neil and even Keith told us how much in love Kevin was. They could not say enough good things about our Livy, and it filled me with pride and joy to know that they felt like this about our beloved girl.

"It's just nice when she's here. She's so bright and cheery."

"I think it's her hair," Neil ventured.

"Her hair?"

We all turned to him with questioning looks.

He blushed a little and turned to his wife for assistance.

"Neil just means that her hair makes her seem even more bright–it's like a beacon. It makes her glow, really. We've never known anyone with such amazing hair, that's all. Anyway, we all just love her and we're so very glad to meet you all."

The meal that Caragh laid out on Thanksgiving Sunday was a feast indeed. She let Mary Honey and me help in the kitchen which was quite nice and companionable–so much nicer than her trying to do it all herself. We bonded very well that Thanksgiving, our first of many.

I thought that she would possibly become friends with Mary Honey–they were of much the same age–but actually, the ones who became quite fast friends and continued with regular correspondence were she and I.

It was astounding to think of finding a friend like that at my time of life. Nonetheless, we seemed to hit it off right away.

What started that aforementioned correspondence was the recipe with the "secret ingredient." She had promised to send the recipe for the fudge cake we had upon arrival at her house and she'd taken down my address quite earnestly. But I am old enough to realize that not everyone follows through on things like this, even if their intentions were well meaning at the time.

However, the week after I returned home I walked down to the end of the lane for the mail and there was an envelope with Caragh McDonald's return address on it.

Inside was a nice note saying how much they had enjoyed meeting us, and how they hoped we would come again, any time, really.

And there, as promised, was the recipe for the cake with the secret ingredient, which did turn out to be a little sinful although probably not as sinful as that homemade brew that Hank had consumed. It was amaretto–four whole tablespoons.

Amaretto Fudge Cake

1 I/4 butter 1 cup flour
1 cup cocoa
¼ teaspoon salt
4 eggs
1 ½ cups chopped nuts [I use pecans]
2 cups sugar
2 ¼ icing sugar
2 teaspoons vanilla
4 tablespoons amaretto [or more, depends on the day]

In a pan melt the butter. Remove from heat and add ¾ cup of the cocoa. Beat until smooth. In a large mixing bowl beat the eggs until fluffy then gradually beat in the sugar until the mixture is quite thick.

Stir in the chocolate mixture and add nuts. Spread the batter in a greased 10x13 pan and bake at 350 degrees for 30 minutes or until firm.

[The timeline is only a guideline, Hannah, you know like those Ten Commandments]

While the cake is cooling, make the frosting by melting a 1/2 cup of butter. Add amaretto and icing sugar alternately and beat until smooth. Beat in 1/4 cup of cocoa and spread on top.

Here's a little extra tip for Christmas at no extra charge:

[This was before the days when people wrote LOL after anything at all but as I am reproducing this recipe I can see that it may well have been inserted here.]

When you serve hot apple cider, serve it with a cinnamon stick, and when you serve hot chocolate, use a peppermint stick.

It was so nice to have you up at Thanksgiving. I don't want to wait until next year for another visit. Burkes Falls is not so very far away, and if I'm not mistaken we will be family one day. So please come again as soon as you can.

With kind regards,

Caragh and Neil."

This was the first time I had seen her name written down, and I was intrigued by the spelling. I decide to write her back and include one of my recipes for her. Most people, of course, were communicating with email by this time and Hank and I were quite able to do this, thanks to endless lessons from Olivia and Mary Honey. We did eventually communicate more by emailing. But I liked that Caragh had taken the old fashioned route of writing out and mailing her recipe to me. I still walked down the lane for the mail every day, and it was nice to get a friendly epistle from that little dark-haired woman.

I replied:

"Dear Caragh,

Thank you for the recipe. I will definitely be trying it in the near future.

I am enclosing two recipes for you that Olivia and I make at Christmas time. She was usually the one who ended up in the kitchen with me and we spent a lot of happy times together there. This one is quite old but I think very Christmas-y because of the peppermint.

No Cook Mint Patties

4 tablespoons butter, softened
1/3 cup corn syrup
1 teaspoon peppermint extract
½ teaspoon salt
4 ¾ cups [about a pound] sifted powdered sugar
I drop each of red and green food coloring

Thoroughly blend butter, corn syrup, extract and salt in a large mixing bowl. Add sugar; mix with spoon and hands until blended smooth. Divide the mixture into three parts. Knead red food coloring into one-third; green into one-third; and leave one-third white. Shape them into little round balls and then flatten them with a fork. Let them dry for a little while and then store them in a tin. Olivia and I add them to little plates that we make up at Christmas.

The second one is peppermint meringue drops [are you sensing a theme here?]:

3 egg whites
½ teaspoon peppermint extract
¼ teaspoon cream of tartar
Food coloring–colors as desired
¾ cup of sugar
White pearl or coarse sugar

Place the egg whites in a large bowl and let stand at room temperature for at least half-an-hour

Beat egg whites, extract, cream of tartar and food coloring on medium speed until soft peaks form. Gradually beat in sugar, I tablespoon at a time, on high until stiff peaks form.

Cut a small hole in the corner of a plastic bag and fill it with meringue. Pipe them out of the bag in little shapes onto a greased cookie sheet and sprinkle with pearl sugar.

Bake at 300 degrees for 20-25 mins. or until set. Turn off oven and do not open the door. Leave them there for one full hour before you take them out.

I hope that you will have a chance to try these out, and if you do, that you'll like them.

I looked up your name as I've never known anyone who spelt their name as yours. I see the meaning of it is "Friend." That's lovely.

Yours truly,

Hannah Moreau."

Some weeks later I received a Christmas card with the postmark of "Burkes Falls" and a warm note from Caragh wishing us all the very best of the season, saying again that we were most welcome to come up for a visit anytime at all. They had a lot of snow and it looked so pretty on the evergreens at the back. She also thanked me for the ornament, which was currently adorning her tree, and she observed that it was "great–just great exchanging recipes."

Agnes took the card from the mantle and read the inside of it as we gathered together by the fire.

"Who on earth are Caragh and Neil? And what kind of a name is that? I didn't know you were in a recipe exchange, Hannah."

This was my sister. She couldn't imagine that I would get a card from someone that she didn't know. I mean, it was different for her–she was out in the big world and knew hundreds of people. But I had stayed right here where everyone who was in my realm of acquaintance she must surely be familiar with.

"Those are Kevin's parents," I explained. "Remember we spent Thanksgiving up there?"

"You were invited, too," Kevin reminded her with a grin. He was not mollified by Agnes' stern manner of speaking.

"Oh, yes. That's right," she admitted. "Anyway, what's this about a recipe exchange?"

"I've heard of cookie exchanges." Mary Honey said. "Why not a recipe exchange?"

"Why not, indeed?" I asked. "Her name, by the way, is Gaelic and it means 'friend.'"

"That's nice," Olivia said. "I didn't know that."

"Well, isn't she more Mary Honey's age?" my sister kept going in her typical manner. Tact and diplomacy had never been her strong points and why would she be any different now? If anything, she was becoming more Agnes-like. "I mean, if she's Kevin's mom."

"Well, of course she is." Olivia said. "But it doesn't matter. There are no recipe exchange age rules."

Everyone laughed. Even, it must be admitted, Agnes herself.

"Anyway," Olivia said loftily, with the air of someone having great news to bestow. "Mom has other fish to fry."

"What does that mean?"

We all turned to look at Mary Honey who had blushed right to the roots of her hair.

"Livy!" She was indeed flustered.

Hank and I looked at each other curiously, exchanging little shakes of our heads to indicate that we were both in the dark on this one.

"Well!" Mary Honey took a deep breath and announced almost shyly, "Mom, Pops, to quote my dearly beloved daughter who can't keep her mouth shut, 'I met a boy.'"

We gasped in surprise and Mary Honey laughed.

"It's not *that* shocking, is it?"

No, no we hastened to reassure her. We were thrilled and when could we meet him?

"Livy's met him. I didn't want anything to do with him if she didn't approve."

Olivia nodded and pronounced him to be "a lovely old fellow."

"He's not that old. He's only two years older than me."

Olivia lifted her hands up, looked at Kevin and said, "I rest my case, Mama dear."

We all laughed again.

"Well, give us the run down." Hank demanded good-naturedly.

Apparently he was a widower and had one son who lived in South Carolina, which is why he was not here at this time. He spent every Christmas with him and his wife and two children. But we could certainly meet him in the New Year. He was a retired teacher at which Agnes gave great approval.

What a happy Christmas that had been, I remembered.

The tree recorded it with a loving ornament from Livy, which she had purchased at my new favorite store in Huntsville and all was calm and bright for us that Christmas Eve.

Kevin was with us, of course and Mary Honey was happy and giggling like a young girl now that her news was out. It was so good to see this. Hank and I had felt an ache in her for a long time. She certainly deserved a stab at happiness.

Boxing Day of that year had been so fulfilling for our family. But half a world away, there occurred the Indian Ocean Tsunami which utterly devastated the eastern coast. I had never heard of that word before and even the school teachers had to admit that they hadn't, either.

It was a terrible disaster that occurred off the coast of Sumatra, Indonesia, and my understanding is that it was caused by an earthquake which triggered other earthquakes as far away as Alaska. Our hearts absolutely broke for those poor people. The death toll was something around 250,000. It was unimaginable.

We all got together and sent money, but it seemed like a drop in the bucket, really.

As I lay in bed I prayed for those people and I asked Mama to watch over them. And then I asked her to keep us all safe. It was only Boxing Day–still the Christmas season. She was my Christmas spirit. I'm sure that she heard me. And I felt safe and warm as I always did thinking about her looking out for all of us, as she had all of my life.

Christmas 2005

Now *that* was a year! I smiled at the warm bundle of sweetness rocking on my lap and told her what a very special year that had been. That had been the year of the wedding. That had been the year of great celebration and joy and love.

We were so attached to Kevin by the next summer that I think Hank and Mary Honey and I [and yes, maybe even Agnes] would have been devastated if he had not become a part of our family. He was so easy and good-natured. But the thing that I loved about him the most was how evident was his adoration for Olivia.

They had told us that they desired quite a small wedding. Neither family had an abundance of close relatives and so after much ado, it was decided to have a small ceremony here at our house and do the old barn up to hold an old fashioned wedding dance. To the dance, the couple was inviting many friends from work and school. There was much to be done, but Olivia and Kevin were undaunted.

"It's a barn dance, Granny. People know that. They don't expect it to be anything but a barn with maybe a few decorations. Leave it to us."

With a great effort I did.

Those were happy, happy times! Busy, oh yes, insanely busy but very joyful.

Caragh and I were as one with the baking and cooking and preparations. I thought that Mary Honey might feel a little left out, but she was so happy with her new beau and so happy for dear Livy that she didn't care how things went down. If we needed help, she would be happy to give it but if we could just carry on without her then she would be forever grateful.

Carry on we did.

We had endless discussions about the menu and the wedding cake–imagine that being left up to us! I thought that Olivia was being very casual about it all, but she just laughed.

"I have complete faith in you, Granny. And in Kevin's mom, too. You two hit it off pretty good, don't you?"

"We really do," I agreed.

She nodded her bright head and smiled.

"Nice," she proclaimed.

"It is."

And it was.

I had turned seventy in June and Caragh was fifty-two, but when we got together we chatted away like a couple of giggly girls.

We had finally decided on a recipe for the wedding cake. Olivia wasn't even sure that they wanted one. But I drew the line there.

"My God, Livy. You have to have a wedding cake."

"Oh, Granny." She hugged me and laughed. "You're so old-fashioned."

"I'll bet Caragh would agree," I told her.

"Oh if you two are going to ban together against me then what choice does the poor bride have?"

"We'll make it, Livy. You tell us what you want and we'll make it."

"Granny, you make it however you think will be the best and it will be perfect."

"No guidelines?"

"No guidelines."

But that proved to be more difficult than ever because of course then we really didn't know how to proceed at all. In the end we decided on a homemade marble cake. Marble seemed like a good choice for someone who couldn't make up her mind–not quite chocolate and not quite vanilla. We made it from scratch and garnished it with royal vanilla icing and flowers straight out of my garden.

Caragh came down from the north for this special cake baking ceremony and actually spent a night at our place. I informed her quite seriously that highway eleven went both ways–north and south. She laughed good-naturedly at this and after making that journey declared that she might just have to make it again.

It was a happy time.

Mary Honey's man, Carl, proved to be an altogether distinguished gentleman who was easy to talk to and easy to be with. He, too seemed to be smitten with our daughter, and after so many years of going it all alone, Mary Honey was happy to have someone to share her life with.

Even now as I reminisce about that year it seems brighter somehow. It stands out as a time of fun and joy for all of us. It was a year for enjoying the friendship and love of new people and renewing the love of our whole family.

Olivia was an absolute vision in her white wedding dress and her red gold curls flowing down her back. Here and there were sprigs of white flowers entwined among those curls. I could see Kevin gasp and tears fill his eyes as she came through the garden path on the arm of her grandfather.

We had both thought that Mary Honey would be the one to give her away but she and Olivia were determined that it should be Hank. He was unaccustomed to being in the limelight, and I thought that it may well kill him, but he managed quite well.

When we made our annual trek to Burkes Falls and subsequently Christmas Tyme in October I was pleased to discover that Bob had a selection of wedding ornaments to mark such an event. I ended up choosing one in which you could put a photo of the bride and groom, and Bob wrote their names and the date and year on it for me. I had purchased it for Livy but I ended up purchasing a duplicate to give to Caragh and Neil. I had plenty of time to shrink one of their photos down and pose it in there for Christmas. I was very pleased with the results.

Olivia was happy to hang it on their first ever Christmas tree beside a little nest that Caragh had sent her.

Apparently it was an Irish tradition to put a nest in your Christmas tree and it was supposed to mean good luck. There was a little poem accompanying it that read:

"Long ago great happiness and good fortune came to those who chose a Christmas tree–a bird's nest in its branches.

Here is a little nest for your Christmas tree–

May the legend come true for you."

Caragh made one for me and Hank as well and I loved it. I had never heard the sentiment before. Mama hadn't been familiar with this custom, although she might have been had we asked her–the question had not arisen.

Olivia also inherited a little star from Caragh, which Kevin had painted as a small boy.

"I'll be as bad as you, Gran, when I'm older," she teased me. "I've got a good start to having a Christmas story tree of my own."

Another venture that Caragh and I had undertaken was to compile a recipe book for Olivia for her first Christmas as a bride. We had endless fun with that one, getting old family recipes and new ones that we tried just to make sure they were edible. A lot of this was done by email, but when we were due to put it all together we purchased a lovely binder entitled "Family Recipes" and made it into something quite spectacular, really. They had so many more things available nowadays than when I was young. I thought this was a great keepsake for a newlywed couple.

Agnes made me promise though–"NO FRUITCAKE!"

And Caragh agreed. I explained that my sister and I were in a constant search to find someone who really, actually did like fruitcake.

The decoration for my tree from 2005 was given to me in a green "Christmas Tyme" box with one of Bob's famous red balls nestled inside. On it was written in white: "Olivia and Kevin: June 11th 2005." It was a thing of beauty and I was proud that I had occasion to merit one of these beautiful shiny balls.

Etched beside the letters was the shape of a heart.

"Why is kissing under the mistletoe believed to be a symbol of peace?"

"Because it used to be believed that if enemies happened to meet under it they would be required to declare a truce for that day and seal it with a kiss,"–at which Kevin pulled Olivia to her feet, dragged her under the doorway and proceeded to kiss her soundly on the lips, making huge, delighted smacking noises.

We all laughed at his antics and I thought for perhaps the millionth time how Mama would have loved these people who had joined her beloved family either by birth or by design. And she would have loved that we had not let go of our Christmas lore.

Now all anyone had to do was to consult "Mr. Googlemaster," as Hank called that popular search engine, to prove a Christmas fact–or any other fact, indeed.

Not so in Mama's time. She had such a lot of information stored inside her head. Her love of everything Christmas made her knowledge base so vast that it was, and still is, unimaginable to me that she could have developed that horrid disease that ate away at her brain until there was no Mama left at all.

If we wanted to know something and she was uncertain of the answer she used to say, "Look it up in your Funk and Wagnall." This was a popular dictionary of the times.

If you were to say that now, I'm sure, people would accuse you of swearing.

The older I become, the more I realize that we were robbed with the early illness and demise of Mama. I am in my early seventies myself now, and I have enjoyed my life to the very fullest. What seems old at one stage of your life gradually does not seem as old when you actually get there. There was so much more that could be done medically now, and I knew that seventy was not considered old anymore. Why, I knew of a local man who was in his early eighties and he'd had heart surgery and was now out and about, as good as new. Another woman of eighty-three had just been started on dialysis over at the new hospital in Brampton. I was unsure if I myself would want to pursue these particular health avenues, but the fact remained that there were definite options in place, and seventy-three was not considered "ready for the scrap heap," as Dad used to say.

I wondered if they had any new medical research in the way of Lewy Body Dementia. I didn't even really want to know. I didn't want to think that if Mama had been born a few years later perhaps her brain damage could have been arrested and she could have been Mama a little longer. Sometimes I think that even a few days–a few hours would have been nice, and sometimes I think that all the time in eternity would not have been long enough.

She had slipped away "betimes." That was another old-fashioned word, and actually Mama herself was the only person that I ever remember using it. She used to say that she'd better get to bed on time or she would meet herself on the stairs in the morning. She was wont to observe that if you were up past midnight then you were up "betimes," and it was the whole next day already. Mama had left us all betimes, of that I was sure.

But we kept up the Christmas trivia. Even if those darned kids would consult their phones and the Internet to make a point, and even if it wasn't the same–how could it be?–we doggedly kept it up.

"What does the word 'wassail' come from?"

"It comes from the old Norse '*ves heil*.'"

"Meaning?"

"Be of good health. And all of the neighbours would visit on Christmas Eve and sing carols and drink to everyone's health."

"Drink what exactly?"

"Usually mulled wine or cider."

"Is there any of that around here?"

I loved the chatter and the back and forth jiving of everyone. Mary Honey's Carl was joining us on Christmas Eve now. He was such a nice man. He was quiet and serious but very pleasant. We grew fond of him mainly, though, because he fulfilled Mary Honey's life so completely. They had been down to South Carolina together and Mary Honey had met his son and their family. It seemed that his son was also pleased about Carl finding happiness after living so many years alone. As a matter of fact, they were heading southward tomorrow after lunch to spend part of the holidays with them.

I appreciated that they stayed for Christmas Eve and the lighting of the way, which had become so dear to us for so many years.

Our group was becoming larger as we walked through the Christmas darkness to light our light. This was a good thing. I was glad to see Carl take Mary Honey's arm. Theirs was a love that was a pleasure to behold. They had both spent years alone and knew how harsh life's journey could be. It was good to find someone who would walk beside you and take your part.

Kevin and Olivia had never wavered in their love and I liked to see them walking arm in arm, their easy affection and conversation flowing from them.

Yet, I could see pain in my dear girl. I could see a hurt in her eyes and I was pretty sure that I knew the cause of it. Not a word had been said but I thought I knew.

My suspicions were confirmed later on that evening.

We'd left our light to shine out in "the Christmas world," as Olivia used to say when she was quite young, and we were returning to the house. Kevin was chatting with Hank and Carl about the best route if there were any impending snow squalls, and Mary Honey and Agnes were discussing school pensions and the best retirement options.

Olivia took my arm and snuggled into me as if she were much younger than her years. I patted her curls where they had escaped from around her toque and were blowing in the December wind.

"Granny! Oh, Granny!"

"I know, honey."

"What? What do you know?"

"I know there's something amiss with you, Livy dear. And I know that it's going to be all right."

"How do you know any of this? I haven't uttered a word."

I paused in my steps and turned to face her on the rugged lane. I touched her young cheek lightly with my mittened hand.

"Because, my darling girl, I've known you since the moment you were born and I know what's in your heart. And I know what you're longing for."

"Really?"

"Yes, really."

She looked down and sighed.

"You're longing for a child–a baby, aren't you, sweetheart?"

She nodded and I saw her eyes glistening with tears in the darkness.

"Oh, Granny," she sighed deeply.

"Another thing that I know–"

She looked up.

"Yes."

"I know why you feel so bad. It's not just the waiting for it, is it?"

"No. It's because of–because of–"

I searched deep into her eyes and I said very softly

"It's because of Baby Holly, isn't it?"

She nodded again. I'd known that for some time now. I knew how close Olivia's heart had been knit to that long ago baby–that baby who would forever be abandoned and lost to us no matter how old she would be now.

"Olivia. Olivia. It's going to be all right. I promise with my whole heart."

"I'm sorry, Granny."

She sniffed and made a stab at regaining her composure.

"Don't you be sorry, dear girl. I am going to lay this problem squarely at the feet of someone who will know exactly what to do."

Olivia smiled.

"Your mama?"

"Yes. My Christmas angel. My Christmas ghost. My guardian angel. Whatever we decide to call her, I know that she shines brighter on this night. On Christmas Eve."

"I'll just leave it to the two of you then, will I?" Olivia was laughing through her tears now.

"Yes. We'll work on it together," I promised her.

And I thought with longing and regret how Mama would have adored this bright, wonderful girl, her great-granddaughter.

"Why was holly believed to be sacred by the Druids?"

"Druids, no less?"

"Yes, indeed."

"Because it was always green and that made them think that the sun never deserted it. Girls in New England thought that if they attached it to their beds that it would prevent the devil from turning them into witches."

Agnes sniffed with contempt.

"Druids and witches indeed."

"It does still constitute Christmas lore, Auntie Agnes." Mary Honey said very sensibly.

"Who died on Christmas Day 1977?"

"I actually know this one," Carl said tentatively. "I can't believe it. I haven't known anything up until now."

Everyone looked at him. None of the others seemed to have the answer ready, so he continued.

"It was Charlie Chaplin. I'm pretty sure."

"That would be right."

"I don't know who that is," Olivia said. "I mean I've heard of him but he died before I was born."

"Well, my dad used to get a laugh out of him. That's why I remember him," Carl explained. "His trademark was a tramp with a toothbrush moustache who always seemed to have a positive attitude in spite of chaos in the world. He died in Switzerland, I think."

"Isn't that where 'Silent Night' originated from? Switzerland, I mean, not Charlie Chaplin."

Again Carl replied with the answer. It was his night to shine.

"I am pretty certain that was Austria."

"Right again, Carl," Kevin whooped. "We'll make a Christmas expert out of you yet."

Carl grinned and held his counsel.

"I remember Mama telling that story. I think that the church organ had broken down or something and they just sang it. It is a beautiful song, but it always makes me a little sad."

Agnes nodded. "If I close my eyes I can still hear Mama singing that song on Christmas Eve," she agreed.

Olivia caught my eye and smiled sadly. I could feel that she had no faith left in my Mama's Christmas power, but I knew differently. I was holding on so tightly and having faith for both of us. Olivia had turned thirty-one in March and with each birthday I could feel the longing grow in her. It was the very worst longing that a woman could have. It was as if you were literally starved for a child to grow within you. She never missed a beat, as she sped through her busy days and gave no indication, ever, of anything amiss in her world. But I was her grandmother. I could look into her beautiful blue eyes and feel her baby-missing heart yearning inside of her.

It was a good year for Canada. In February Team Canada had won a gold medal when Sidney Crosby scored an overtime goal against the US of A. Hank and I were not big hockey fans but we were certainly fans of our beloved country. There was a great deal of cheering and roaring all over the nation and even in our small corner of the world.

There was a Christmas ornament for that and it was very significant. It was Kevin who saw to that. We had decorations proclaiming all sorts of events and by God the Team Canada win was not going to pass our tree by. He and Olivia laughed as they hung it up.

"Your granddad would have liked that," I told her. "He always cheered for the Leafs, but they haven't won the Stanley Cup for a while."

"1967," Hank observed dryly.

"Well, all right. Quite a while," I was forced to admit. "But he would have loved that Team Canada won a gold medal. I'm glad you two got that one."

"My God, Hannah," Kevin exclaimed. "I've never known anyone ever with as many decorations as you have. Some of these are like antiques."

"They're not *like* antiques." Hank said. "They bloody well *are* antiques."

"Like us," I told him.

We all laughed as we gathered together and sorted out our red Olympic mittens to brave the cold night.

That was last Christmas Eve. I couldn't believe it, really. I had used up all of the evening hours thinking of Christmas Past and now here I was recounting last year already.

I thought fondly of Kevin and how firmly ensconced he was in our country lives. He fit into our family as if there had been a chair there at the old wooden table with his name written on it, and all he had to do was slip into it. It is so nice when things work out like that. I hadn't known at the beginning how he would feel about these Christmas Eve walks, but the long and the short of it was that where Olivia went then Kevin went, too. And so he had donned a scarf and toque in our old kitchen the first year he came with us as if it was the most natural thing in the world, and took Livy's arm as he prepared for our outing. He looked a little silly in his multi-colored toque, but he laughingly explained that you needed one up where he came from unless you wanted frostbite on your ears. His brother, it seemed had actually had this and it was most unpleasant.

I was grateful to this boy for so graciously allowing us the luxury of having our Livy with us for Christmas Eve and part of the big day. She was happy when he was here, and we were all happy when Livy was here. A great arrangement, I thought to myself. Winnie the Pooh might well have a quotation that would work in this situation.

The only thing that they needed to complete their lives was something that I was working hard at. If love and prayers from her grandma and her Great-Grandma Angel/Spirit/Ghost could do it, then we would try our utmost.

And so last year, I gathered the candle and jar and matches and, taking Hank's arm, we set off on our annual walk, with Kevin now quite familiar with our tradition.

He walked arm-in-arm with Olivia, eagerly leading the way for Hank and me, Mary Honey and Agnes and Carl. I could hear her chattering as it floated back to me on the night wind. Her words were happy and her tone was gay as she spoke of how she loved this candlelight tradition. I could feel with all of my heart that this might very well be her blessed year.

Kevin sure is a great fellow, I thought to myself, dreamily walking along beside Hank, thinking as I did every year of my loved ones and of Mama and Danny.

I didn't realize right away that a car had stopped at the side of our concession and a man had emerged from the driver's side. He seemed to be talking to Olivia and Kevin but I couldn't hear their conversation. I guess I just figured that he was requesting directions or the like.

Then I heard Olivia say, with a hint of apology in her voice,

"This is my Grandma and Grandpa–Hank and Hannah Moreau. Granny, Papa, this is Ken Johnston."

"Hello," I said and Hank nodded his head by way of introduction. I had no idea what this stranger was doing stopping at our lane on a bitter cold Christmas evening.

He stepped a little closer to us and peered at Mary Honey.

"I'm Mary Honey," she said dubiously. "I'm their daughter. Is there something I can do for you?"

Her tone was just a little sharp but Ken Johnston seemed unaffected by this.

He had the air of a man who had come on a mission and he was going to fulfill that mission no matter what. The trouble was, I had no idea what he wanted. I could see by Hank's expression that he was no wiser that I.

"I want to tell you something," he started. His voice was shaky but determined.

"Yes–what would that be?"

"You are the family of the boy who was killed down on the four corners of Norval quite a few years ago, are you not?"

"Thirty-five years."

My tone was hollow. It sounded foreign to my own ears.

"Yes. I wanted to tell you that–that–"

"Yes, Mr. Johnston. What exactly would you like to tell us?"

Mary Honey had stepped closer to him now and her words were clipped and cold in the night air.

"Please listen–"

"We are listening."

The man took a deep breath and looked around at our small group. He was not a very big man. He was quite ordinary-looking actually, with glasses and round features. He was probably close to our age–not a young man, then.

What on earth did he want?

"The night that your son was killed it was me who ran over him in the car."

He said this all in one breath and after the words were out he sighed deeply.

"You were drunk!"

This came from Agnes who was trying to get a grasp on this whole event unfolding before our eyes.

"No. No. I hadn't had a drop to drink. The drunk was the one who smashed into the car your son was in and caused the accident."

I was still in the dark, but Hank and Agnes were starting to nod their heads. I could see comprehension dawning in their eyes.

"You were the second man," Hank said softly.

"Yes, sir. I was. I would give anything not to have been, but I was the next one–the second man, as you say."

"The second man?" Mary Honey sounded as mystified as I myself felt.

Hank turned to her and spoke very gently about a long ago hurt and tragedy that we wore on our souls every living day.

"When Danny was killed they were never sure if he died on impact or if he died from being run over by the next car that came along. They knew that his neck was broken but they weren't sure which happened first. They didn't know as much about these things then as they do now."

"He wasn't wearing a seat belt, I guess," Olivia said very softly.

I didn't realize that the exact details of her uncle's death had never been explained to her.

"Well it wasn't the law then, you see." Ken Johnston looked at Olivia and spoke again.

"They were in the newer cars, of course, but not as many folk had new cars as they do today. It was not unusual to ride around and not wear one, especially if you were close to home."

Olivia nodded and I could see that she felt uncomfortable.

But Ken Johnston continued with determination.

"I've wanted to talk to you for years and years but I've never had the opportunity, and I've never had the nerve to just march up to your front door. I live in Huttonville just around the corner so I often pass this way. At least it used to be Huttonville till these big developers got ahold of it. Anyway there isn't a day goes by that I don't think about that boy of yours."

We were all silent now and he carried on. His words were crisp and clear and seemed to hover in the cold atmosphere.

"I was driving down that hill and I hadn't really realized what had happened before I felt a bump under my front tire."

I gave a little sob out loud but caught it before it turned into a cry.

"I'm sorry, ma'am. I'm so sorry. I got out of the car and ran to him but he was already dead, you see. I would have given anything to help him but it was just too late for your boy. I wanted to kill that drunk with my bare hands. And I would have, too, if it would have brought your boy back. He was such a small boy. I wasn't even sure what I had hit when it first happened."

His voice broke now, too, and I found it in my heart to feel compassion for him.

"No," Hank agreed and his tone was almost dreamy. "He wasn't very big for his age. He never really got too big, you see."

There was a huge silence then–an all-encompassing silence that seemed part of the night and the stars and the velvet darkness.

Ken Johnston shifted uncomfortably and nodded to us.

"Well, I'll let you good people go now. I've held you up long enough. I'm sorry if I brought up bad memories tonight. But I've wanted to tell you since that night how sorry I am and how I'd give anything–" his voice broke now but he continued, "anything at all really if that had never happened."

He looked around our little circle and turned to go.

"Mr. Johnston!"

It was Mary Honey who took a step towards him as he walked away. She had stepped away from Carl who had been holding her hand and watching her with concern.

Her eyes were blazing–even in the darkness I could see the fire in them. My Mary Honey who had emerged from the eye of Hurricane Hazel and had fire in her soul–who had been marred forever when she lost her beloved brother that fated night.

I held my breath.

"Mr. Johnston!"

He turned expectantly until his gaze rested on her, standing apart from us.

"Yes."

She sighed deeply and held out her hand to him.

"Thank you for stopping to tell us that. It wasn't your fault, you see. But," she sighed, " it's just never, ever been the same without him."

He took her hand and held her in an embrace for a brief moment.

"I can't even imagine. Please know that I don't forget him either."

"Thank you," she whispered.

He turned and left.

She turned and walked into Carl's waiting arms. Then Olivia went over and wrapped her arms around them both. Kevin came and embraced them and the three of us old folks did the same.

Mary Honey laughed feebly.

"Group hug," she said weakly.

"Sounds good to me," Kevin said and made us laugh by adding, "That's what we do in Burkes Falls."

And so we stood in a circle of love under the stars last Christmas Eve, a little stunned after this emotional encounter. It felt odd to think that we had barely known this man existed but yet he had wanted to meet us for all of these long years.

And so, forgiveness was our Christmas gift last year.–a gift that was difficult to find when remembering the night of Danny's death. My heart stuck a little in its relentless rhythm as I thought of Mary Honey finding it within her.

But I knew that it meant everything to Mr. Ken Johnston.

I could see it in his eyes as he hugged my daughter.

And I heard it as he called out, just before he stepped into his car,

"God bless all of you people. And Merry Christmas!"

In unison we all called back, waving our red mittened hands,

"Merry Christmas, Mr. Johnston."

So that's my Christmas story. It is told and retold every year as I ponder the branches of my tree–as I take my Christmas memories out, one by one, and I dust them off and recall them. It is not a very remarkable story–quite ordinary actually–but it is mine. Someday maybe Baby Hannah will be happy to know of it.

I looked around the tree, searching in its branches between the glowing lights until I found this year's round red Christmas Tyme ball that hung there proudly. I had been waiting a long time to see it. But not too long. I could still enjoy it and all it stood for. Thank God that I was still healthy and able to rock this darling child and tell her about her ornament. *Bob had done a good job as always*, I thought as I read the white letters boldly standing out on the shiny red:

"Hannah Mary Holly 2010."

Beneath her name Bob had painted a little holly leaf.

The greatest gift that anyone in the world can ever receive is the gift of a new baby into the family at Christmas time. I would have been happy to rock in that old, worn rocking chair all night and gaze into the sweet, clear face of my new great-granddaughter. I could have smelled her beautiful pure smell and kissed her chubby body until the whole season passed. But of course, there's always work to be done, and that is not practical.

Maybe, though, I could rock a little longer–just a little.

I was growing fanciful in the half-light with only the soft glow of my beloved tree to see by. I was thinking of how people say that Christmas is getting very commercial with each year. When I hear this I always remember Mama saying [because, oh yes, they were saying the same thing in Mama's time], "Christmas is only as commercial as you choose it to be. We must try to find it in our hearts and in our joy."

Mama was so wise. She knew that Santa was really a spirit of kindness and giving, and she knew that Christmas was above all else about love. She lived this in her own loving ways.

Mama always said that Christmas Eve was a magical time. People would stop and help others–push them out of the ditch, help those in need–Mama believed that this was the true meaning of Christmas. One Christmas Eve she remembers someone in Norval giving a coat to an elderly man who was shivering in the cold. She used to cite this as an example of the good in mankind. Mama always believed in that inherent goodness.

The entire world seems to have IPods and phones and blackberries now, but I remember when people did not always look down at what was in their hands but up–up at the beautiful sky and stars above.

Oh, dear, I'm sounding like an old lady. Well, in truth I *am* an old lady now.

I think back to the days when the old phone hung on the kitchen wall and you had to listen for the ring to know if it was for you or the family up the road. And we baked the old-fashioned way with love and laughter and flour everywhere.

In a few short days we will make that familiar trek down the lane with our mason jar and our candle and lots of long matches. Our group is growing and that fills me with undefinable joy. That is the way it should be, I think.

There will be Hank and I and Agnes–of course–where else would she be, my dearly beloved only sister? Mary Honey and Carl will be there, too with Olivia and Kevin, and there will be a new December baby to attend. She may have to be wheeled in a stroller, as there is not as much snow as there once was, but we will bundle her up and we will glory in the sight of the beautiful Christmas glow reflected in her perfect blue eyes.

I look back on all of the lights we left for Christmases from my whole life long, and I think of how each year was dependent on all of the others. How they all fashioned a string of brightness, which fills up the calendar of my years. I felt as if I could well have hung bits of my heart on the tree for the worst years–the years of loss,1975 and 1980–but somehow I survived. And I'm still surviving.

The candles of my Christmas Eves are a shining vista illuminating my life. I was so sad when I lost Danny and Mama. I thought that I might die without them. But there is an unexpected gift that old age has brought to me. I feel these loved ones closer each year. I feel that it won't be too long now that I will be with them. Danny will be healthy and Mama will be clear-minded and I will be complete at last. Each Christmas brings me closer to them.

And Mary Honey and Carl and Olivia and Kevin will make new traditions with a new wonderful Hannah.

So to all of you dear readers who were kind enough to buy this little book and are reading it tonight, I wish you a very happy and blessed Christmas.

Try always to leave a little Christmas light shining in your heart. Even a small one can make such a difference.

I hope that everyone out there can find some solace and comfort in the Christmas spirit–whoever you profess him to be.

And so,

Good night.

Merry Christmas, everyone!

The End

CPSIA information can be obtained at www.ICGtesting.com
Printed in the USA
LVOW080619300513

336031LV00003B/33/P

9 781622 123124